WANTING MORE
THAN FINE

"Call me Jim. Please." His left hand in his pocket,
he holds his right hand out to me.
As though we're equals.
"Thank you, Doctor—I mean—just Jim," I say.
He chuckles. "Haven't done anything yet."
He *has*.
No older man ever invited me to shake hands.
No other adult ever asked me to call them by name.
He even said "please" although I'm a patient.
A smile tugs at face muscles I haven't used for a while.
My hand slips into his
as though it remembers his touch
and we've held hands often
in a previous life.

"Think it over," he says. "Take as long as you need."
I let my fingers stay in his pale palm
like brown roots sinking into chalky white soil. "I'll do it."
"Good," Dr. Murali says. "He'll have you walking fine in no
time."

"I don't want to walk fine.
I want to dance."

ALSO BY

Padma Venkatraman

The Bridge Home

Island's End

Climbing the Stairs

A TIME
TO DANCE

A TIME TO DANCE

Padma Venkatraman

PENGUIN BOOKS

PENGUIN BOOKS

An imprint of Penguin Random House LLC, New York

First published in the United States of America by Nancy Paulsen Books, 2014
Published by Speak, an imprint of Penguin Random House LLC, 2015
Published by Penguin Books, an imprint of Penguin Random House LLC, 2020

Visit us online at penguinrandomhouse.com

THE LIBRARY OF CONGRESS HAS CATALOGED THE NANCY PAULSEN BOOKS EDITION AS FOLLOWS:
Venkatraman, Padma.
A time to dance / Venkatraman, Padma.
pages cm
Summary: In India, a girl who excels at Bharatanatyam dance refuses to give up
after losing a leg in an accident.
ISBN 978-0-399-25710-0 (hc)
[1. Novels in verse. 2. Dance—Fiction. 3. Amputees—Fiction. 4. People with disabilities—Fiction.
5. India—Fiction.] I. Title.
PZ7.5.V46Ti 2014
[Fic]—dc23
2013024244

Penguin Books ISBN 9780147514400

Printed in the United States of America

Design by Marikka Tamura
Text set in Goudy Oldstyle Std.

15

As this book neared completion,
I was struck by the story of a dancer
—Adrianne Haslet-Davis—
who had a limb amputated
as a result of the Boston Marathon bombing.
This work is dedicated to the courageous people
I've been privileged to meet and those whom
I'll never be honored to know,
whose spirit triumphs over terror and tragedy.

A TIME TO DANCE

PROLOGUE

TEMPLE
of the
DANCING GOD

Clinging to the free end of Ma's sari,
I follow the tired shuffle of other pilgrims' feet
into the cool darkness of the temple,
where sweat-smell mingles with the fragrance of incense.

Pa's hand rests heavy on my curls.
The priest drops a pinch of sacred ash into Ma's palm
and she smears it on my forehead
above the red dot
she paints between my eyebrows each morning.

I push through the rustling curtain of women's saris
and men's white *veshtis*,
tiptoeing to see better.
A bronze statue of Shiva,
four-armed God of dance, glistens.
He balances on His right leg alone,
His left raised parallel to earth,

the crescent moon a sparkling jewel He wears
in His matted hair.

Carved high into the temple's granite walls
are other celestial dancers.
"Pa?" I tug at my father's shirt.
He lifts me onto his shoulders
but the sculptures are
too far away to touch.

After the crowd empties out
into the sunshine of the temple courtyard
I, alone,
slip back
into the soft blackness of the empty hall,
spot a stepladder propped against
my dancer-filled wall,
and climb. Up, up, up, to the very top.
Leaning forward, I trace
dancing feet
with my fingertips.

"What are you doing, little one?" A priest
steadies my ladder. "You don't have to climb ladders
to reach God.
He dances within all He creates.
Come down."
I run my fingers

along the curve
of each stone heel.

The priest's laugh rumbles up into my ears.
"Place a hand on your chest.
Can you feel Shiva's feet moving inside you?"
I press on my chest. Feel bony ribs. Under them, thumping,
faint echoes of a dance rhythm: *thom thom thom.*
Shiva outside me, gleaming in the temple sanctum.
Yet also leaping, hidden inside my body.

"God is everywhere. In every body. In everything.
He is born at different times, in different places,
with different names.
He dances in heaven as Shiva, creator of universes;
He lived on earth as Buddha,
human incarnation of compassion;
and as you can see, He moves within you.
Now, please, come down, little one."

I'm halfway down the ladder when Pa and Ma rush back in.
Pa prostrates, laying his squat body flat on the stone floor,
thanking God.
Ma thanks the priest,
words of gratitude bursting from her like sobs.
"Searched—the other four temples—couldn't find her—
so scared—what if she'd left the temple complex—
run outside the walls—into the city—"

As we leave, Ma's thin fingers pinch my shoulders
tight as tongs roasting rotis over an open flame.
Pa scolds, "You could have burst your head
climbing a ladder like that!"

My head is bursting
with images
of stone dancers come alive, the tips of their bare toes twirling,
with sounds
of the tiny bells on their anklets twinkling
with music.

A TIME TO DANCE

HOPING
and
WAITING

I race upstairs,
kick my sandals off outside our front door,
burst into our apartment. "I'm in the finals!"
My grandmother, Paati,
surges out of the kitchen like a ship in full sail,
her white sari dazzling
in the afternoon light that streams through our open windows.
I fling my arms around her.
Drink in the spicy-sweet basil-and-aloe scent of her soap.
Paati doesn't say congratulations. She doesn't need to.
I feel her words in the warmth of her hug.

"I knew you'd make it." Pa plucks me
out of Paati's embrace into his arms.
"Finals of what?" Ma says.
I've only been talking
about the Bharatanatyam dance competition
for months.

Mostly to Paati, and to Pa, but Ma's hearing is perfect
and we don't live in a palace with soundproof walls.

Paati retreats into the kitchen.
Paati's told me she doesn't think it's her place
to interfere with her son and daughter-in-law.
Pa's eyes rove from Ma to me.
He's caught in the middle as always.

Ma's diamond earrings
—the only reminder of her wealthy past—
flash at me like angry eyes.
"Veda, you need to study hard.
If you don't do well in your exams this year—"
For once, my voice doesn't stick in my throat. "I am studying hard.
To be a dancer.
I'm not planning to become an engineer. Or a doctor."
Or any other profession Ma finds respectable.
Ma launches into her usual lecture. "Dancing is no career for a
middle-class girl.
You need to study something useful in college so you can get a
well-paid job."
I sigh extra-loud.
My dance teacher, Uday anna, isn't rich. But
his house is larger than ours.
Clearly, he earns more than
Ma at her bank job and Pa at his library.

Ma goes on and on.
Back when I was younger, I'd struggle to be better at school
for Ma's sake.
But numbers and letters soon grew too large for me to hold
and I grew far away from them
and Ma grew out of patience.

Paati places steaming *sojji*, my favorite snack, on our table.
The sweet, buttery smell of cooked semolina is tempting
but I leave the plate untouched.
March into the bedroom Paati and I share.
Slam the door.
Pa knocks. Says, "Come out, Veda. Eat something."
"Leave her alone," Ma says. "She knows where to find food if
she's hungry."

I probably shouldn't have slammed the door.
But Ma never even said congratulations.
She's never pretended my dancing made her happy.
But never has a performance mattered more to me
than being chosen for the finals of this competition.

All my life, Ma's been
hoping
I'll do well at science and mathematics
so I could end up becoming what she wanted to be:
an engineer.

All my life, I've been
waiting
for her to appreciate my love
of the one thing I excel at:
Bharatanatyam dance.

SPEAKING
with
HANDS

"Steps came to you early. Speech came late," Paati said.
She'd tell how she watched me pull myself up by the bars
of my cradle at eight months,
eager to toddle on my own two feet.

Months before others my age, she said,
I could shape thoughts with my fingers.
My body wasn't shy.
While words stumbled in my throat
losing their way long before they reached my lips,
like lotus buds blossoming my hands spoke my first sentences
shaping themselves into *hasta mudras*:
the hand symbols of Indian classical dance.

Paati said, "It was as if you remembered
the sign language of Bharatanatyam
from a previous life you'd lived as a dancer
before being reincarnated as my granddaughter."

Paati always understood everything I said with my hands.

DANCE
PRACTICE

I'm a palm tree swaying in a storm wind.

My dance teacher
sits cross-legged on the ground,
tapping beats out on
his hollow wooden block with a stick.

I leap and land on my sure feet,
excitement mounting as Uday anna's rhythm speeds,
challenging me to repeat my routine faster.
My heels strike the ground fast as fire-sparks.
Streams of sweat trickle down my neck.
My black braid lifts into the air, then whips around my waist.

Nothing else fills me with as much elation
as chasing down soaring music,
catching and pinning rhythms to the ground with my feet,
proud as a hunter rejoicing in his skill.

The climax brings me to the hardest pose of all:
Balancing on my left leg, I extend my right
upward in a vertical split.
Then I bend my right knee, bring my right foot near my ear,
showing how, when an earring fell off as He danced,
Shiva picked it up with His toes
and looped it back over His earlobe.

Locking my breath in my chest to keep from trembling,
I push myself to hold the pose
for an entire eight-beat cycle.
A familiar thrill shoots up my spine.
I enjoy testing
my stamina, my balance.

Uday anna's stick clatters to the floor. He claps.
"Pull that off and you're sure to win."

Both feet on the ground again, I pirouette and leap,
rejoicing in the speed at which
my body obeys my mind's commands,
celebrating my strong, skilled body—
the center and source of my joy,
the one thing I can count on,
the one thing that never fails me.

LONE PALM

Kamini, my rival,
enters the classroom as I leave.
I extend my hand, saying, "Congratulations.
Heard you made it to the finals, too."

"Thanks," she says, sharp as a slap.
Sweeps past me,
ignoring my outstretched palm.

I want to tell her I truly think she's a wonderful dancer,
convince her we could be friendlier though we compete.
But as usual, the sentences I want to say
collapse in a jumbled heap in my brain.

I'm a lone palm tree
towering over grassy fronds of rice in a paddy field,
yearning to touch the sky although
I get lonelier
the higher I go.

TIME

Returning home after dancing, I trip
on the first step
of the shared stairwell of our apartment building,
one of thirty identical concrete high-rises built
to house lower-middle-income families:
teachers, accountants, librarians, bank tellers, clerks.

Mrs. Subramaniam, who lives in the apartment below ours,
calls out from her open door, "Careful!
You don't want to twist your ankle."
Shobana, her youngest daughter—
who's a little older than me—waves.
I nod at them, too tired to move my tongue.

When we were younger
and Shobana's now-married sisters lived at home,
I'd see them at play in the street, running and shouting.
Mrs. Subramaniam would come upstairs and say, "Veda, go out.
Join their fun."
"Soon," I'd promise.
But I preferred to stay inside, dancing alone,

tiptoeing, twirling,
feeling as light as a jasmine's white petal
as my feet flitted across the floor
and time slipped away . . .
Too happy to stop
until darkness fell
and the street was empty.

BADGE
of
HONOR

Paati's sitting cross-legged on the floor
in front of our household altar.
When she sees me, she stops chanting
and puts her prayer books away.
My head pounds
like it's the ground beneath a dancer's feet,
my shoulders hurt from holding my arms upright for hours,
my thighs ache.
Paati gets a bowl of pungent sesame oil.
She brushes back the wet curls that cling to my forehead
and massages the dark oil into my scalp.

"I've got pain in muscles I didn't know existed."
Paati knows I'm not complaining.
Pain is part of the path to success.
Pain is the passion
of muscles burning to be best,
the flame that rose within me
when I conquered my vertical split,

awaking a store of strength
lying unseen beneath my brown skin.
Pain is proof
of my hard work,
proof of my love for dance.

GIVING

I love seeing happy creases form around Paati's eyes
when she watches me dance.
She leans forward, her wicker chair creaks,
her body sways,
attentive as a snake
following the motion of a snake charmer's pipe.

Though I'm still tired, I say,
"Want to see what I practiced today?"
Before Ma and Pa return, I want to give back to Paati
the story she told me as a child,
the story I'll perform at the competition:
of how Shiva once competed at dance with His wife.

I try to make my dance appear effortless
though it isn't,
the way Paati makes everything she does for me look effortless:
cooking my favorite dishes,
helping me with homework,
combing knots out of my long curly hair,
massaging my muscles until her touch chases my aches away.

THE MUSIC
of
APPLAUSE

My trembling fingers pin the free end of my dance sari
over the left shoulder of my blouse.
One last time I stretch each leg out, flex and point my bare feet,
wiggle my toes to ease tense muscles.
Every seat in the auditorium is filled.
The air twangs with expectation like a veena's taut string.

Last of twelve competitors,
I'm hiding behind the wings, waiting.
I watch Kamini finish up her routine.
She twirls in a tight circle and comes to a stop,
bare feet to the sides, knees bent outward,
holding a diamond-shaped space between her legs.
As Kamini walks offstage,
Uday anna's mouth shapes the harsh words
"Not fast enough,"
though she looked flawless to me.
Kamini's lips quiver, but I have no time to worry about her.
I'm next.

The velvet curtain,
crimson as the thick lines of *alta* painted on my feet,
shudders apart.
Hands at my waist, I march out
keeping perfect time to the crisp, clear commands
of Uday anna's cymbals.
The rows of brass bells on my anklets
vibrate to the rhythm of the *mridangam* drummer.
My skin tingles as I step into the music,
give in to the icy thrill of pleasure
that spreads through me whenever I dance,
the pleasure of leaping into a cool lake on a sweltering day.

The music swells and strengthens like a flood.
Waves of song pulse through my body.
I love portraying Shiva,
who, through the steps of His eternal dance,
creates and destroys universes.
I whirl across the stage,
stop to balance on one leg,
holding the other behind me with both arms,
my body bent outward, bow-shaped.
A burst of applause encourages me.
Steps quickening, I build to the climax.

A rope of anxiety and excitement twists in my stomach
as I assume the most daring pose in my routine:
my vertical split.

What if I don't "pull it off"?

I must. I will.
I hold my pose.

Frenzied clapping breaks out,
applause so sweet and strong I can taste it,
sweet and strong as South Indian coffee.
A fresh bolt of energy shoots through my veins
as I hear the music of a crowd
clapping just for me.

DANCING
My Body
BEAUTIFUL

A judge's voice echoes over the microphone.
"This year's winner
impressed us with her flawless technique.
She brought alive poses rarely performed.
In honor of her speed and skillful mastery over her body,
we present this year's prize to
Ms. Veda Venkat."
Uday anna beams. "Ten years I've waited for this honor. I knew
you'd win."

So dizzy with joy I feel almost off-balance,
I return to the stage,
where three judges line up to congratulate me.
One of them hands me a small bronze image of Shiva dancing,
a replica of the deity I first saw as a child
in the temple of the dancing God.

Clutching Shiva to my chest,
I thank the judges.

Strangers crowd around me as I exit the stage.
A tall, skinny boy elbows through the crowd,
extends a hand toward mine, looking hopeful.
Behind him, two more boys gaze awestruck
in my direction.
I whip around, expecting to see
my best friend, Chandra, nearby,
whose dimpled chin and sparkling talk
inspire a love-struck longing
in nearly every boy we encounter.
Surely, these looks are meant for her.
No one stares at me
this way.

I don't see Chandra anywhere.

I once read an article about beauty in a magazine.
I measured my nose to see if it was long enough,
if my eyes were large enough,
if my lips were thick enough
to be beautiful.
They weren't.

One of the boys stutters, "Ms. Veda, you-you're
—awesome."
Behind him, another boy echoes, "Awesome."
I fight to keep my lips from breaking into a silly grin.

The eager pressure with which the boys grasp my hand
tells me
my graceful movements make up for
my incorrectly proportioned face.

I can dance beauty into my body.

JOYS
of
WINNING

My best friend, Chandra, pushes through the crowd,
slaps my back as though our team just won a cricket match.
She pulls my hand up into the air.
I let it linger there.

We were about eight years old
and I was standing at the edge of the cricket field
when Chandra's bat lofted the red cork ball
in my direction.
Eyes scrunched up against the glaring sun, I raced after it.
Felt the ball's leathery hide in my palm.
Raising an index finger, I signaled she was out.
Chandra ran over. I was scared she was angry.
"Great catch, Veda." She pumped my hand.
I couldn't believe Chandra—
good at everything yet also popular—
knew my name.
Chandra slid an arm across my shoulders.
"From now on," she said, "you're on my team."

Playing cricket with Chandra,
the sun baking my black curls
until they feel as hot
as a piece of fire-toasted chappati bread,
I like the sweet swish of the ball landing in my hands,
the crack of my bat sending the ball high into the sky.
But neither sound fills me the way dance does.
Winning at cricket doesn't compare
with the joy of winning at dance.
A joy that makes my heart beat
to a brisk, victorious tempo:
tha ka tha ki ta
tha ka tha ki ta.
A joy that makes
rhythmic music swirl in my ears.

BLACK DOT

The crowd parts to let Pa through.
He throws his arms around me.
Says, "Splendid, simply splendid."

Ma says, "Congratulations."
For a brief moment I hope for more, but that stiff word
is all
she gives me.

Paati presses her wrinkled cheek next to mine. Whispers,
"You'll have other chances to win over your ma."
Ma forces a smile. I return it.
Paati's right. Already, Ma's at least trying.
And my career's only begun.

Ma's tight face is like the small black dot
dancers paint on their left cheeks to ward off the evil eye:
enough only to blemish my joy for a second,
too tiny to take away from the thrilling certainty
of a future filled with success.

LOST

After waving Chandra and my family good-bye,
I return to bask in Uday anna's praise,
speak to the judges, and answer reporters' questions.
I pose for photographs
until my eyes hurt from the sea of flashing cameras.

Hours later, changed out of my dance clothes,
I climb into the van that's waiting to take
dancers, teachers, and musicians
home.
As I settle into a seat behind the driver,
Kamini climbs in.

She walks past me without a word of congratulations,
cozies up with our lanky drummer a few seats back.
Her voice floats into my ears,
". . . Veda's dance . . . technically okay but emotionally flat
and spiritually lacking,
don't you think?"

Kamini—of all people—talking about spirituality!
Nearly every day when we were children
she'd whine and pester Uday anna:
"How long must we only move our feet?
When can we wear jewelry?
When can we wear silk dance dresses?"

But maybe I
have
been dancing differently
since I first started performing onstage.

Have I lost
the kind of joy
I felt dancing as a child?

The van lurches forward.
My thoughts race back.

BACK WHEN

Pa said,
after our pilgrimage to the temple of the dancing God,
I tried balancing one-legged—imitating Shiva's pose—
over and over until my bruised skin
was as green as Goddess Meenakshi's.
So he took me to Uday anna.
Uday anna drummed his hairy fingers on his desk,
worrying I was too young.
Pa said, "Test her.
See how well
she keeps time."
Intrigued, Uday anna sat cross-legged on the floor.
Tapped out the simplest beat:
thaiya thai, thaiya thai,
one two, one two,
right foot, left foot, right foot, left foot.
My feet followed his rhythm.
He set more complex steps.
My feet matched his tempo.
To Pa, he whispered,
"Yes."

As a child,
the rhythmic syllables of Bharatanatyam beats
spoke a magical language that let me
slip back
into the awe I first felt
when I touched the celestial dancers' carved feet
on our pilgrimage to the temple of the dancing God.
Maybe my dance lost depth
as I gained height.

Then
as I danced
the world grew big, wondrous, beautiful.
Time melted.
I disappeared.
Now
I twirl so fast
the world vanishes.
Only I exist.
Then
everywhere, in everything, I heard music.
Music I could dance to.
Now
is the music I long for most
the music of applause?

SPEED

Our van rampages down the potholed road
like a runaway temple elephant.
The driver presses the red rubber horn, trumpeting it nonstop,
like every other insane driver in Chennai city
always in a hurry.
Usually it drives me crazy, the useless sound of horns,
the unnecessary speed.
Tonight, the roller-coaster ride provides the exhilaration I need
to stop brooding.

Strangers showered me with praise.
Boys craved
my attention.
Who cares what Kamini says?
I clutch the seat in front of me,
pretend I'm a kid on the giant wheel at the Chennai city fair,
pretend I'm flying
every time the van hits a pothole and throws me into the air.

The driver
swerves.
Monstrous headlights from another vehicle
glare at us.
Brakes screech. Metal grinds against metal.
My body careens sideways.
I see the trunk of a pipul tree looming.
A gray giant
coming closer.
Closer.
"Shiva! Shiva!" someone screams.
A man's voice
rasps out a swearword.
"Stop! Brake!" Uday anna shouts.
I hear Kamini's terrified wail. "Aiyo! Aiyo!"
Shattered shards of glass
scatter moonlight.

Pain
sears through me
as though elephants are spearing my skin with sharp tusks
and trampling over my right leg.
The seat in front, torn and twisted,
pins my body down.

Uday anna struggles to lift the crumpled wreckage
of the mud-spattered seat.

The drummer tries to wrench
my trapped body free.
Kamini stares
down at me, shudders,
turns away, retching.
I smell
vomit.
"Don't look," Uday anna cries, laying a hand across my eyes.
Through his fingers I see
shredded skin, misshapen muscles. Mine.
Feel sticky blood pooling
below my right knee.

Pain swings me away.

The stench of burnt rubber.
Flashing lights. The hysterical wail of an ambulance.
Garbled voices.
Cold. Mangled sounds made by masked figures.
Darkness.

WAKING

Each breath is an effort.
Every part of my body aches.
The air stinks of ammonia.

I push my heavy eyelids open.
Above me
patches of paint peel off the ceiling.
Bandages scratch at my skin.
An IV tube sticks into my left arm.
I struggle to sit up.
"Let me do that for you. Lie back."
A nurse
starts cranking up the back of my
hospital bed.

Against the wall, Ma sits dozing.
Beyond Ma, a glint of steel—
a wheelchair.
Fear slices through my dull brain.
No. The wheelchair
cannot be mine.

I see an ugly bulge under the sheet covering my legs.
Yank off the sheet with what's left
of my strength.
My right leg ends
in a bandage.
Foot, ankle, and nearly half of my calf,
gone.
Chopped
right off.

"No!" The nurse pulls my sheet
back over the leftover
bit of my right leg.
But I still see the
nothingness
below my right knee.

Ma jerks
awake,
leaps up from her chair,
runs toward me.
Her eyes scared as a child's,
she clutches the metal rail
of my hospital bed.
"I'm so sorry," she says.
"About
everything."

I turn my face away from Ma,
away from the cold metal gleam of the wheelchair
in this puke-green hospital ward.

Outside the window, I see the gnarled trunk
of a huge banyan tree.
Its thick branches sprout roots that hang down
shaggy as Shiva's hair.
Wish I could slide out like a cobra.
Hide amid those unkempt roots.

"You were in a van," the nurse says. "The driver was speeding.
A truck crashed into the van and ran it off the road.
Your driver hit a tree. He died.
Remember any of that?"
A pipul tree's pale trunk
coming closer and closer.
Screaming.
The smell of vomit and blood.

"Your surgeon, Dr. Murali,
did all he could to save your foot.
He is a great surgeon.
He tried to save it but
he had to amputate.
Your foot was
too far gone."

My hands thrash at the sheets.

I feel the nurse's vise-grip around my wrists.

"Calm down. No need

to panic. You're young. You'll recover in no time.

Dr. Murali even had a physiatrist advise him during the surgery

on making the best cut

so an artificial leg would easily fit.

You're lucky to have Dr. Murali for a surgeon."

Lucky?

Ma reaches for my hand, whispering my name.

I squeeze my eyelids tight. Shut out everything.

No no no no no.

I need to get away.

Can't.

Trapped.

EMPTINESS
FILLS

Pa comes in. Holds my hand.
His fingers are wilted stalks.
Drooping.

Tell me it's a bad dream, Pa,
please.

"Just stepped out for a cup of coffee. Didn't mean to leave you.
Didn't want you to find out this way—we
—they—tried—" he chokes.

He moves his lips.
No words come.

My eyes are dry sockets in a skull.
Pa and I share
emptiness.

EVERYWHERE,
in
EVERYTHING

Everywhere, in everything, I used to hear music.

On sunny days when I was little, after Ma and Pa left for work,
we'd walk to the fruit stall down the road, Paati and I.
There was music
in the drone of horseflies
alighting on mangoes ripening in the heat.

Each day of the monsoon season
the rhythm of rain filled me.
Rain on the roof, rain drizzling
into rainbows of motor oil spilled by scooters and rickshaws,
silver sparks of rain skipping
across waxy banana leaves.

Every morning I'd wake to the *krr-krr-krrk* of Paati
helping Ma make breakfast in the kitchen,
grating slivers of coconut for a tangy chutney.
I'd dance *thakka thakka thai*,

into scents of cumin, coriander, and red chili.
Wrap my arms around Paati's plush body.
At night I'd hear music
in the buzz of hungry mosquitoes
swarming outside my mosquito net,
in the whir of the overhead fan
swaying from the ceiling.

In the gray-green hospital room
silence
stretches.

ASHES

Light fades. Night falls.
But darkness doesn't shroud the sight
of my half leg
from my mind's unblinking eye.

Under the sheets my hands reach
like a tongue that can't stop playing with a loose tooth.
Over and over the rough bandages my fingers run,
trying to smooth over
reality.

In the morning I feel Paati's hands kneading my temples.
Not even her touch soothes me.

Murmuring a prayer,
she places the bronze idol of Shiva I won at the competition
on my bedside table.
"*Mukam karothi vachalam; pangum langayathe girim.*"
God's grace moves the mute to eloquence
and inspires the lame to climb mountains.

I glance at my dancing Shiva,
His left leg raised parallel to the earth,
His right leg crushing the demon of ignorance,
His inner hands juxtaposed, palms flat,
His outer hands
holding aloft the fire of creation and destruction,
and a drum
keeping time to the music of His eternal dance.
I try to repeat Paati's prayer. I strain my ears to hear
His music.

It feels like Shiva destroyed my universes of possibility,
like He's dancing
on the ashes
of my snatched-away dreams.

NAMELESS

"Veda, you've got a roommate," a nurse announces.
A woman with a mop of gray hair
gives me a yellow-toothed smile.
"I heard you lost your leg. How?"
I don't want this stuffy space invaded.
Especially not by a chatty old woman.
I don't answer.
"Talking will help you heal, you know.
They cut my toes off. Diabetes.
Now tell me about you."
I give her more silence.
"What's your full name, girl?
Veda what?
You can tell me that, at least, hmm?"
No.
I don't know who I am
anymore.

PAIN
UNCONTROLLED

Nurses come and go,
black strands of hair escaping bleached white caps,
flowing saris peeping from beneath starched coats.

"Pain under control?" they ask.

As a dancer, how carefully I mastered
the mechanics of my body—
learning to bear just enough pain
so I could wear it proudly, like a badge of honor.

I want to tell the nurses no scale can measure
the pain of my dreams
dancing
beyond reach.

PINS, NEEDLES, PHANTOMS, *and* PAIN

The nurse pulls the faded privacy curtain around my bed
to keep me partially hidden
from my roommate's curious eyes. Why bother?
The curtain isn't soundproof.

My surgeon, Dr. Murali, lists my injuries in a tired voice,
his limp hair matching the glint of his silver-rimmed spectacles.
Below-knee crush injury, concussion, two cracked ribs,
cuts on thighs and shoulders.
"Nothing more."
Sounds more than enough to me.

My once-golden-brown skin
mottled with more blue-black bruises than a rotting mango.
My once-strong body
bandaged in so many places

I feel like a corpse someone started to mummify
and abandoned halfway.

"Will I have scars?"
"None a sari won't hide."
My sigh of relief is cut short
by a stab of pain from my cracked ribs.

Dr. Murali says, "You may have phantom pain.
You might feel the part of the leg you lost
is still there.
Many patients say it feels
like when a part of your body falls asleep
and later the numb part wakes up with a prickling sensation.
Like pins and needles.
Except it hurts worse."

Pain from the ghost of a leg that's gone,
adding to the excruciating ache
in my existing limbs?
Just what I need.

He continues, "Most patients get over it soon.
A year or two at most."
Maybe when you've got
hair as gray and glasses as thick as he does
two years feels like a short time.

When my roommate and I are alone, she says,
"Sometimes they cure ghost pain
by cutting more off."
Butcher what's left of my leg?
No, thanks.

ALL I
STILL HAVE

Paati says, "You have your whole life
ahead of you.
You have
me, Ma, Pa, Chandra.
And God.
God is within you, Veda. So is His strength."

I don't feel God is anywhere nearby,
let alone inside me.

"Your grandpa was a wonderful man," Paati says.
"When your pa was a baby and I was widowed,
I fell from the heights of being
a joyful young wife and mother
into a dark valley of sadness.
I could have stayed there.
My in-laws wanted to look after me.
They were loving and kind.
And working widows were rare in my day.
But I didn't dwell on what I'd lost.

I returned to college, became a teacher,
grew independent.
Because I chose to focus on all I still had:
my son, my intelligence, my supportive in-laws."
In the past, Paati's spoken of my grandpa.
But until now I never realized
how much she loved the man
her parents made her marry.
And how unusual and brave Paati was.

As she leaves the room Paati says, "Doesn't mean it was easy.
I still miss your grandfather. I think of his kindness every day.
Some things you never get used to being without."
Like a right leg.
Like moving effortlessly everywhere.
Like dance.

FINDING *My* VOICE

A nurse enters, carrying a sponge and a basin.
She draws the privacy curtain around my bed and starts
undressing me
as if my body belongs to a doll she owns.
My body is not hers.
It's mine.
I still have
most of it.

"What are you doing?" I'm surprised
I sound strong enough to make her step back.
"Sponge bath." The nurse's voice wavers.

"I can do it myself.
I've got arms."

I'm finding my voice
though I've lost my leg.

EXPERIMENTAL
PROJECT

Dr. Murali is followed into the room by a strange man
with flame-gold hair and bright blue eyes.
Is my pain medication making me hallucinate?

"We're lucky," Dr. Murali says, "to have, working with us,
Mr. James, from America,
who is collaborating with an Indian research team
to create cost-effective modern prostheses.
He's agreed to help with your rehabilitation
and with the fitting and making of your prosthesis . . ."
He suggests I'm lucky, too, to be part of the project,
because my family doesn't have enough insurance.

I feel the American's eyes on me,
looking
as though I'm more than an amputee, a number, a chore.
He crosses over to me, his strides large, a broad smile on his lips.
"Veda? Did I say your name right?"
"Yes, Doctor."

"Call me Jim. Please." His left hand in his pocket,
he holds his right hand out to me.
As though we're equals.
"Thank you, Doctor—I mean—just Jim," I say.
He chuckles. "Haven't done anything yet."
He *has*.
No older man ever invited me to shake hands.
No other adult ever asked me to call them by name.
He even said "please" although I'm a patient.
A smile tugs at face muscles I haven't used for a while.
My hand slips into his
as though it remembers his touch
and we've held hands often
in a previous life.

"Think it over," he says. "Take as long as you need."
I let my fingers stay in his pale palm
like brown roots sinking into chalky white soil. "I'll do it."
"Good," Dr. Murali says. "He'll have you
walking fine in no time."

"I don't want to walk fine.
I want to dance."

The American—just-Jim—lets my hand go,
but his gaze holds me.
His eyes, blue and bright,
light a sparkle of hope inside me.

LESS UGLY

I used to dream of handsome men
whose touch
made my skin tingle.

In the hospital's airless exercise room,
I hurt from deep in my ribs to the surface of my skin
when handsome Jim lifts me out of the wheelchair,
helps me hold on to parallel bars
to do the simplest of movements—
bending and straightening,
moving what's left of my legs.

"You're doing great, kiddo," he says.
I don't feel great.
My shameful croaks of pain
grate on my ears, harsh as a frog's.
But when Jim says "great,"
rolling the r's around like melting sweets
in his American mouth,
when he calls my lopped-off leg a "residual limb,"

when he says I'm a person with a disability,
not handicapped,
when he's nearby, using his kinder words,
he makes me feel
a little less ugly.

VISITORS

Chandra visits wearing a wobbly smile,
with her wet-cheeked ma
and her pa, who clutches her ma's shoulder
for support.

I watch Chandra walk across the green tile floor,
her strong, muscular cricket-captain legs gliding toward my bed.
She takes no notice of where slopes and cracks
hinder a wheelchair ride.

Chandra says,
"Can't wait for you to get on the cricket field."
I don't care about cricket.
All I want is to dance again.
She should know.
She tries, "The whole team's waiting for you to get back."
—A polite lie I never expected
to hear from my best friend.
I hardly ever spoke to anyone on the team except Chandra.
She says, "I miss you in class, too."
I say thanks.

Our conversation totters
close to the cliff of silence.
Keels over.

Chandra says, "See you
later."
Not see you
soon.

I try to lift my eyes to meet hers.
But my gaze stays low
and follows her quick, sure steps
across the uneven floor.

After she leaves, though I shut my eyes,
I can't stop picturing
the ease
of her walk.

STAYING AWAY

Uday anna
doesn't visit.

He's fine, Pa says, when I ask.
No one else was badly hurt.
Except the driver, who died.

After ten years of seeing Uday anna
every day after school,
I can't believe he doesn't miss me
enough to visit
once.
Tomorrow he'll come, I keep thinking.
Tomorrows come and go.
He sends a card:
"With wishes for a complete recovery."
As if I could ever be
complete
with one leg half gone.

His absence shows
he thinks I'm too crippled to dance again.
I tear up his card.

I'll show Uday anna.
Sooner than he thinks,
I'll be back in his classroom,
back in competition,
back on my own feet.

Or rather,
back on my own
one
foot.

WHEELS
SHORTEN

I avoid looking at my chopped-off lump of leg uncovered.
When nurses change my dressing
I stare at the banyan tree outside.
But when I navigate in "my own special wheelchair"
—rigged with a pad to keep my leg elevated—
I can't not see
this broken bit of my body that I hate.

Chandra hates her flat chest.
Chandra's eldest sister hates her fat thighs.
I never found myself beautiful
until the day I won the dance competition
but I loved my strong body anyway.

Stuck in a wheelchair,
I'm waist-high to everyone else.
Or worse,
lower than even that.

FORWARD

Pa, Ma, and Paati are in the hospital room
when Jim strides in with a pair of crutches.
Jim says, "Got a feeling you weren't too keen
on wheelchairs. Or walkers.
Thought you might prefer to leave the hospital on these."
"Yes!" I can't wait to stand dancer tall.
Move without rolling on wheels.

Jim's eyes sparkle at me. "We'll need to practice.
Especially going down stairs. Come."
Pa says, "Won't crutches hurt her ribs?"
Jim reassures him it's okay.
Ma touches my shoulder, then draws back quickly,
as if she's scared I'll bite her hand off.
I don't like Ma acting so unsure of herself.
I almost prefer the old Ma, who'd argue with me.

Paati pats my cheek, like she used to when I was little
and I fell down and hurt myself.
Her firm touch tells me she expects
I'll get up without a fuss.

She leaves me no choice
except to get off the bed,
lean on my crutches, and try.

Bowing low as though I'm a princess,
although I must look as ungainly as a clown on stilts,
Jim says, ceremoniously, "I'll hold the door, ma'am,
while you walk through."

My ribs jolt with pain and my shoulders feel raw
but I return his grin.

And
I go
forward.

NICKNAMES

My crutches carve wide circles in the air.
"Veda, can you lift and plant your crutch tips?
Please don't swing them."
I plant crutch tips ahead, pull forward
with my body and
what remains of my legs.

As Jim guides me
on my new mode of travel, I get him to tell me
how he first came to India.
"On a trip to see the desert in Rajasthan, in the north,
with an ex-girlfriend."
I'm glad to hear
the girlfriend is past tense.
He continues,
"Fell out of love with her
but stayed in love with this country."
I wonder how many girlfriends he's had.
Don't ask.
"Beautiful place, Rajasthan," he says.
"Pink palaces, hundreds of years old,

women wearing skirts with bits of mirrors sewn on,
camels burping in the middle of city traffic."
He wrinkles his nose up as though he can smell them.
I smile.
He says he went to an Indian hospital
where they gave amputees free prostheses,
and that got him interested in making artificial limbs.
This project was a way for him
to travel to India again and use his expertise to help people.
He tells me he loves travel, loves new challenges,
loves people.
I've never met another older person
as friendly, as open, as carefree.

I refuse to rest until he forces me to turn back, saying,
"Let's not overdo it, kiddo."
"I'm not a kid," I rasp.
"Aye, aye, ma'am." Jim salutes with one hand in his pocket.
I start to laugh
but my ribs remind me I still have healing to do.
Grinning despite my pain, I say, "That's better."

After that, Jim mostly calls me ma'am.
And even when he says kiddo, I stop minding.
Because whether he says kiddo or ma'am in his teasing tone,
the corners of his eyes crinkle,
and I feel singled out and special.

FAMILY
DISTANCES

Two of Pa's cousins
whom we rarely see
come all the way from Bangalore city, a half-day train ride away.
They say they're sorry about my accident,
then talk politely with Pa and Paati about other relatives.

Ma's family probably doesn't even know I'm hurt.
Paati told me they disowned Ma when she married Pa,
even though he was Brahmin
and they were a lower caste,
because he was a poor librarian
with no prospects of getting rich,
and they were wealthy.
Ma never
speaks about them.
Her diamond earrings are all we have to remind us
of them
and their riches.

MY *Last* VISITOR

After Pa's cousins leave,
someone I expect even less appears:
my former rival, Kamini.
Holding a big bunch of red zinnias.
Why is she here?
To gloat over my crutches?

Hands shaking, she thrusts the zinnias in my face.
"For you," she says, pointing out the obvious.
I'm so shocked I open and shut my mouth twice, fish-like,
then manage to mumble, "Thanks."
"So- so- sorr-rry," Kamini stammers.
What's Kamini scared of? She's the one with a sharp tongue.
My tongue's never been quick enough to answer back.
My foot won't outpace her feet anytime soon.
"Sorry," she repeats, looking so uncomfortable
I start feeling more sorry for her than irritated.
"Kamini? Not your fault."
Her face contorts as though she's being tortured.

She stumbles on her way out of the room,
leaving me wondering why she came.

"Your friend?" my roommate asks.
"Nice red zinnias she brought."

"Not my friend." I consider
tossing the flowers into the wastebasket
where I threw our dance teacher's torn-up card.

But Kamini actually visited,
which is more than Uday anna did.
As we're not exactly friends,
and seeing how she was shaking the entire time,
it must have been hard for her to come.
Kamini's flowers deserve better treatment
than our dance teacher's worthless card.

I put the red zinnias on the side table
between my roommate's bed and mine
so she can enjoy them.

DISCHARGE

Dr. Murali removes most of my bandages.
My cuts and bruises are healing.
He says I can go home with my right leg still bound,
stitches still in.

"Maintain good posture.
Bad habits are hard to break," Jim reminds.
He guides me one last time,
up and down a flight of stairs and through the corridor.
He stays at my side.
I hobble behind Ma, Pa, and Paati,
glad I'll soon be free of innumerable pairs of nurses' eyes.
Scared I won't be near Jim's caring arms,
won't hear him say, every day,
"You're doing great."

Near the main doors, I see two nurses, heads together,
sharing my story
in too-loud voices.
"She was a dancer, that one."
As though I'm a star in some sad soap opera.

Not "was."

Am. Am. Am.

I move past the nurses, my crutches tick-tocking on the tiles

like the pendulum of an old clock.

Not quite a dance rhythm.

Yet.

RETURNING
to
NORMAL

Squashed between Paati and Ma in the backseat of a taxi
speeding farther and farther away from the hospital,
my stomach shrinks fist-tight with fear
as a bus overtakes us,
passing so close by I could touch it if I reached out the window.
My palms feel wet.
Sweat, just sweat. Not blood.
A lorry honks, coming at us,
speeding on the wrong side of the road.
Dust clouds fly into my eye through the open window.
The smoke makes me gag.
I tense,
though I feel Paati's fingers massaging the back of my neck,
trying to calm me.
I hear Ma say, "Please drive slower. Be careful."
"Don't worry, madam.
Ten years I've been driving in Chennai city traffic."

The driver screeches to a halt
in the middle of the concrete jungle where we live.

Our apartment building looks unwelcoming as I enter.
Clutching my crutches, I stand at the bottom step,
thinking through the motions of climbing on crutches.
Feeling alone. Frightened.
Far from Jim's encouraging voice.
Missing his strength, his support.
Missing the safety of the hospital.

Pa says, "Veda, would it be easier if you leaned on me
and left your crutches behind?"
Maybe,
but I say, "No."
Ma pulls anxiously on an earlobe.
Her diamonds scatter the sunlight.
Paati nods. Her nod says, "You can do it."
I plant my crutches on the ground,
propel my body upward.
My leg reaches the first step.
Then, my crutches join me.
Pa says, "Don't worry. I'm behind you."

"How is Veda?" Mrs. Subramaniam shouts.
I want to yell, *Ask me. The accident didn't damage my ears.*
Her shout brings other neighbors out.

They crowd on the landings or lean out their doorways,
watching me labor up the steps
of our shared staircase.
They make me feel as if
I'm the star attraction
at a freak show.

GECKOS,
GHOST CRABS,
and
REGENERATION

Lumbering at last into the bedroom I share with Paati,
I collapse on my bed.
A gecko stares at me,
its large eyes almost popping out of its sockets.
Waving its yellow-brown tail from side to side
like an admonishing finger,
it chirps, "Th-th-th."
I shake a crutch at the gecko. "Shut up!
I'm going to dance again!"
Clucking with fear, it turns tail and scurries
toward the open window.
Before racing onto the branch
of the pipul tree that brushes against the windowpane,
the gecko drops its tail on the sill.
Feeling slightly sick, I watch the dismembered part
seesawing up and down—as if alive—
while the tailless gecko disappears up the tree.

Once, at the beach, when I was a child,
Ma pointed at tiny ghost crabs scuttling along the seashore
and said, "If one leg is bitten off by a predator,
crabs can regenerate that lost leg."
Pa added, "Geckos can regrow their tails."
I thought—how magical,
how wonderful.

Paati comes in and places my Shiva statue
on the table between our two beds.
I want to throw it out of the window
at the gecko that's chirping loudly
as if to brag about powers
it has
and I lack.

SOUNDS
of
LAUGHTER

Chandra drops in,

apologizing for having been away so long. "I was busy."

"Busy doing what?" I demand.

She sighs. "Okay. I wasn't busy. It's just

I don't know if it helps when I visit."

"I don't know either."

"I feel I should come."

"Coming to see me on my sick bed is your duty?"

"So what if it's a duty?" Chandra shakes her head. "Don't friends

have a duty to each other? Don't you see I want to help?"

"I hate seeing you walk," I say.

It's a relief to finally confess that.

And relief to hear

Chandra snap, "Fine. Sit and stew in your self-pity."

But then, softening her tone, she goes on,

"Sorry. I understand how you feel."

"You can't understand, Chandra."
"True. I guess I can't imagine
being in your
shoes."
I snort with laughter. "You mean my one
shoe?"

Chandra looks frightened.
I giggle and tell her,
"You look as scared as that night Paati told us a ghost story
and you had to run to the bathroom three times."
"Five times," Chandra corrects.
A mist-thin giggle escapes her.

My ribs must be healing.
Laughing doesn't hurt.
That realization sends me into another peal of laughter.

Our laughter thickens
into a fog
filling the room.
It's a little forced, a little hysterical, but it's good to feel
connected.

DRESSING

I lock the door to my room.
Balancing on my crutches, I open my dresser.
Inside, neatly folded, sit my school uniforms:
Western-style blue collared shirts to go with gray skirts
or embroidered cotton *kurti* tops with loose *salwar* trousers.
Can't dress or undress standing,
so I sit on the bed, wriggle into salwar trousers,
hop on my crutches and force myself to look
at something I've avoided so far:
my full-length reflection
in the long mirror on our wall.

A one-legged girl stares back.
She isn't me! a voice screams in my head.
She isn't me!
Letting my crutches clatter to the floor, I fall back onto my bed.
Not me!
I punch my pillow.
Not me!
Punch. Punch. Punch.

Not me!
A new voice whispers,
Be grateful you can still stand.

On crutches I face my mirror-self.
Dare to stare
lower down.
One trouser leg flaps emptily below my bandaged limb.
I try on my long school skirt and my bandaged limb
juts out below the hem.
I whip my skirt off. Crush it. Fling it on the floor.
Toss all my school uniforms on the ground.

In an open drawer, I see
the blue batik skirt Chandra and I bought
before my accident.
I brush my cheek against it. The skirt still smells new.
Haven't worn it once.
My tears soak into the silky fabric.

Paati knocks.
Trying not to think how good the skirt
would have looked on me,
I shove it in the bottom drawer.
Pile my other suddenly too-short skirts and dresses on top.
Wipe my face dry with the back of my hand.
Unlock the door.

Paati casts a look at the crumpled heap of clothing.
Picks up a skirt. Examines it.
"I could let out the hems," she offers.
"Your skirts can be lengthened quite a bit."
"Thanks, Paati. Thanks so much. Thank you."
She pats my cheek. "You tell me
when I should shorten them back."

I nod
sure she'll never need
to shorten my skirts again.

CRIPPLED

Pa begs to escort me to the bus stop
although I've been riding the public bus to school
alone every day since I was ten.
He worries
drivers won't stop long enough
for me to get safely in and out.
He wonders if we should arrange a taxi.
As if we can afford taxis on a daily basis.
I reason with him. "We're at the end of the bus route.
The bus is always empty when I get in."
Ma says, "Veda, please, we don't want you—"
"You don't want me doing things by myself anymore?"
That gets me my way.

When I arrive at the bus stop,
a little girl bounces over, her pigtails bobbing.
She addresses me politely,
calling me older sister—*akka*.
"What happened to your leg, akka?"
She looks too young
to realize her question is rude.

"Accident." I thrust my crutches as far ahead as I can,
distancing myself from her wide-eyed curiosity.
A man with a pencil-thin black mustache
leans out of a window.
"What happened to your leg?"
My throat hurts as if a thorn's stuck in it and I ignore him.
The bus's steps look steeper than I remember.
I hesitate on the ground,
trying to picture Jim standing next to me,
his cheerful voice teaching me how to climb on crutches.
An old woman
greets me from her usual place in front,
"Girl? How did you lose your leg?
An accident? Or a disease?"
"She's not telling," the man says.
"So rude she is being. In our day we always
answered our elders."
The woman sighs. "Very true. Very true."
As fast as I can,
I get away from them, to the back of the bus.
Stare out the window,
sensing innumerable eyes staring at me.
Someone taps me on the shoulder.
The khaki-clad bus conductor.
He's seen me in his bus nearly every school day.
I wait for him to ask
the question.
He only says, "Good to have you back."

Hands me my ticket and moves on.
I want to hug him.

The bus jerks onto the road.
A temple elephant lumbering along in a procession
obstructs traffic.
I'm thankful it slows the bus down
at least for a short while.
Soon the bus is hurtling madly
through crowded streets.
I press back into my seat,
clutching my schoolbag.
Sweat plasters my skirt to my thighs.
My stop feels light-years away.
By the time we arrive, the bus is packed.
"Let the lame girl through," a lady shouts as I struggle to push
through the crowd.
She sounds as though she's trying to be helpful.
My face flushes
hot with shame
as I navigate carefully
down the steep steps
and out of the bus.

LOOKS

Clunking along the bleak school corridors,
I must look as asymmetric
as a heron balancing on one leg.
I wish it wouldn't take Jim so long to make my prosthesis.
I hate announcing my arrival on crutches
—stomp, clomp, stomp, clomp—
loud enough to make every head turn in my direction.

When lessons are over
everyone pours out onto the sports field.
"You could coach us, Veda. Please? Come?" Chandra pleads.
So I go.
The other girls from the cricket team gather around me.
A few mumble that they're sorry,
their nervous eyes politely stuck to my face,
wary of accidentally straying too low and catching a glimpse
of the space beneath my right knee.
Some welcome me back in extra-bright voices,
saying it's nice I'm back
though they hardly know me.

Silent, shy, following Chandra,
at school, I was her shadow.
Only at dance did I shine in my own light.

Listlessly
I listen to girls whack at the red cork ball with willow bats.

Mekha, a vicious girl, who plays so well
Chandra's forced to keep her on the team,
walks past me.
"Hey, Veda, I was pretty lame today. Wasn't I?" She giggles.
Her twin, Meghna, peals with laughter.
As they walk away, I hear Mekha say,
"Veda's so sensitive!
Are we supposed to stop using certain words
because she's handicapped?
Should we give cricket stumps
a new name now that she has a stump?"
The girls fall on each other, laughing some more,
and their taunts echo loudly in my head
long after I leave the field.

NAMES

Chandra stops by in the evening. "Why did you leave early?
Without telling me?
What happened? I was worried."

Words spill out of me, fierce as tears.
"I'm sick of being a cripple.
I hate hearing people talk about me.
And even when they're not talking about me,
ugly words are always around:
stump, lame, handicap."

"If people are calling you names, I'll take care of them."
Chandra makes fists.
"You're just more advanced than we are.
I saw this TV show about how, maybe, in a hundred years,
we'll all have implants to make our bodies stronger."

I slap at a crutch. "This isn't an implant.
It only enhances my weakness.
I'm going to drop out of school."

"Veda, you never give up.
Not even at cricket,
which you don't care much about.
You know why our team won so often?
Because you inspired me.
However desperate a match seemed,
I could read in your face
that you refused to accept defeat."

She's right, but her words surprise me.
"How do you know?"

"Maybe others can't see your feelings.
I, however, have X-ray vision." Chandra makes a funny face,
sucking her cheeks in and rolling her eyes.

My teeth feel stuck together
like I've been chewing cashew candy,
except my mouth tastes bitter, not caramel sweet.
It's work to get my jaws unstuck and laugh
but I'm used to challenging the muscles of my body.
I do it for Chandra's sake. Because friendship is about laughing
when the other person is joking to make you feel better.
Even if you don't find her joke all that funny.

EXPOSED

Dr. Murali removes my stitches.
I make myself stare
at my
bare
residual leg.

As healed as it ever will be.

Below my knee, above where my leg now ends,
a grotesque smiley mouth leers at me:
a C-shaped scar.

Looking at my uneven skin
exposed
hurts
worse than salting a fresh wound.
Closing my eyes, I turn
away.

Dr. Murali sings the praises of prostheses so enthusiastically,
it's as if he's encouraging

Ma and Pa to cut off their legs and replace them
with "marvelous" artificial limbs
that are "so much stronger" than our own.

Dr. Murali says, "We will give you a shrinker sock
to compress your limb
into a conical shape so it'll fit easily into your prosthesis.
Wear it as much as you can over the next month
so your limb doesn't become
dog-eared or bulbous.
Roll antiperspirant on the skin beneath your sock
so the area stays dry. Keep it clean.
We don't want it getting infected and smelly."
My cheeks burn with embarrassment,
as if I've been playing cricket in the heat.
Bad enough having Jim
see this part of me, naked,
without imagining it
dog-eared, bulbous,
stinking, swollen, disgusting.

Jim kneels by my foot
so close I could rest my chin on his golden head.
"Hey there." Jim's normally buoyant voice is soft.
One of his knuckles, rough as a cat's tongue,
brushes against my inner thigh
as he helps me pull on my "shrinker sock."
His accidental touch tickles,

sending an uncomfortable flutter through my stomach.
"Veda? I'll make you a leg you can dance on."

I feel dizzy as if I'd stood up too fast,
though I get up slowly on my crutches.
Dizzy at the sight of him kneeling by my foot,
dizzy at the thought of Jim and me alone in his office,
his dazzling eyes watching me dance
on the leg he's promised he'll make me.

IN
the
EYE

I'm at the table finishing my homework
when I glimpse Paati in our kitchen
wiping beads of sweat off her brow
with the edge of her white sari.
"Paati, let me help."
"I was going to make you some *uppuma*."
"I'll cook my own snack. You do too much for someone your age.
Chandra's grandmother sits in front of the TV all day."
"Don't criticize your elders," Paati says, but her eyes twinkle.
"Paati, I'd never criticize you. You've done so much in life."
"Didn't you tell me Chandra's grandmother
raised eight children? I only had one."
"You raised Pa all on your own!
You became a schoolteacher!
Most widows of your time didn't dare leave home!"
"Finish your homework."
"Done." I stuff my books into my schoolbag,
clunk over to help her.

"Veda, you look tired. Go and rest. I enjoy cooking."

"I'm not tired," I lie.

"I'm old, not blind," she says.

"I wish my classmates were blind.

And the people who ride my bus, too."

I warm a blob of clarified butter in a pan.

The smell of melting butter fills our kitchen.

I toss in some black mustard seeds.

They crackle. The sound reminds me

of Mekha and Meghna cackling. "Everyone stares at me.

All the time.

Everyone looks at Chandra, too,

except that's because she's pretty.

In my case, it's because I'm not."

"Chandra's pretty," Paati says. "And so are you."

"Only if I'm dancing."

"Veda, onstage you sparkle with confidence.

But your body doesn't transform

offstage.

Your curls are just as long,

your back just as straight,

your figure and face just as lovely.

Your hands flutter whenever you talk. And you

move so elegantly.

As delicately as a butterfly flitting between flowers."

"Not on crutches, I don't."
"All
the
time," Paati says.

She's my grandmother.
No wonder she believes I'm always graceful.
Beauty, as the proverb says, I now understand,
is, indeed, in the eye of the beholder.

WHO DANCED
Ahead
OF ME

"Did you get those just because of me?"
I motion at the rows and rows
of books on Bharatanatyam
stacked on Jim's bookshelf,
in his sunny workroom on the third floor of a redbrick building
on the forested campus of the technology institute
right in the middle of the tar-and-concrete maze of Chennai city.

"You bet, kiddo."
The hair on Jim's hands is powdered white
from the plaster of Paris
he's mixing with water
to make a mold of my residual limb.

I can't believe he's taking so much time to learn
about what I most love.
I feel flattered—more than flattered—by his interest.
I want to say how deeply

his care and dedication touch me.
Instead, all I do is sneeze from the dust Jim is stirring up.

Jim motions at a wall.
"Got those in your honor, too."
Posters of three dancers, all
one-legged.

"Let me introduce them to you, ma'am." Jim points
at a handsome man wearing a suit and shoes.
"He's an African-American tap dancer.
They called him Peg Leg Bates. He danced with a wooden leg.
Way back in the 1920s and '30s."
Next, Jim shows me an Indian man named Nityananda,
dancing a classical style similar to Bharatanatyam.
Nityananda balances on one leg, his residual limb hidden
beneath the graceful drapes of his white veshti,
his upper body naked except for his golden dance jewels,
his arms raised, palms together above his head,
eyes closed.
But it's the third dancer
off whom I can't take my eyes:
a dark-haired, round-faced Indian lady.
"Sudha Chandran," Jim says.
"She danced your own beloved Bharatanatyam
with a simple, inexpensive artificial limb
created in India: the Jaipur foot.

The prosthesis I saw on my first trip to India
that inspired me to design artificial limbs.
We'll be making you a far more modern leg
with greater flexibility and range of motion."

I dream of my picture
hanging next to Sudha Chandran's on Jim's wall.

As if he can read my mind, Jim says,
"One day, kiddo, I'll add your poster to my collection."
I love hearing the pride in his tone,
love his certainty,
love how he
hears my unspoken words.

BEGGAR

Paati and I go to the Shiva temple near our home.
She walks slower than usual.
We pause in front of a small vacant lot
so she can catch her breath.
"Paati, are you feeling unwell?"
"Just age catching up with me," she says.

An old beggar, almost bent in two,
shuffles out of a ragged tent in one corner of the lot.
He holds out hands skinny as a chicken's feet.
Paati drops a coin into his palms.
"God bless you," he says to her.
Then he turns to me. "And you, too,
so you aren't a cripple in your next life."

Outside the temple wall,
Paati takes off her slippers.
I don't.
I'm not sure I want to limp in.
"Angry with God?" Paati says.
"Why shouldn't I be, Paati?

Why did He take away my leg?
Why did He make that man so poor?
Is God punishing us for sins we committed
and bad Karma we built up in a past life?"
"I don't believe in a punishing God," Paati says.
"I believe in a compassionate God.
To me, Karma isn't about divine reward or retribution.
Karma is about making wise choices to create a better future.
It's taking responsibility for your actions.
Karma helps me see every hurdle as a chance to grow
into a stronger, kinder soul.
When I was widowed, I was angry and scared
but I used my anger to act braver than I felt.
Everyone believed my act and soon I believed it, too.
I truly became a brave and strong teacher.
Maybe when you feel angry,
you should try pretending you're onstage,
let anger fuel you into acting a part from a dance-story,
a part that could help you."

I leave my lonely slipper
next to Paati's pair
and follow her.

Inside the temple, the scent of sacred camphor
mixes with the acrid smell of bat droppings.
My eyes flit to the dark corners of the cavernous ceiling,
where bats hang upside down.

There are no dancers
on this temple's walls.
Here, even Shiva
stands still.

Paati surrenders herself to prayer, neck bent, eyes closed.
Sensing Paati's conviction He exists,
I feel some comfort.
But I wish I could find a way
to worship that would fulfill me,
as Paati's firm faith in prayer seems to fill and strengthen her.

For a moment, my childhood memory of the deity
in the temple of the dancing God
blazes so fiercely I feel the heat of the flames
He holds in one of His four arms.

I miss
the blissful ecstasy of the dancing Shiva
I saw.
Whose music I heard
as a child.

ACTING ANGER

At the bus stop, I hold my head high.
I'm not a bride of long ago
being forced into marriage with someone she doesn't know.
I'm not a widow of long ago
whose world is circumscribed to a circle at her feet.
I'm the granddaughter of a woman
who was brave.
Who used her anger.
Who told me to treat the world as my stage.

I hold myself as straight as I can on crutches.
Pretend I'm the legendary Queen Kaikeyi,
whose strength in battle impressed King Dasharatha
so much
he begged for her hand in marriage.

I stare down the first nosy stranger
who questions me.
He's a lowly subject
of the kingdom I rule.

The bus
is my royal chariot.
I return every curious glance
with my imperial glare.
No one dares pester me.

On my way out of the bus,
I poke through the crowd with my crutches.
The old woman who sits up front jerks her chin at me.
"You there. Girl.
When are you going to tell us how you lost your leg?"

My regal stance must not scare everybody.
I bare my teeth in a too-wide grin.
"Crocodile bit it off."
My sarcasm is lost on her.
She bends toward me.
"How exactly did that happen?"
"Like this." I thrust my face next to hers, open my mouth
and snap it shut. Crocodiles don't growl, but I roar, "Grrrr."

The woman shrieks and
a ripple of laughter spreads
as I stride down my royal staircase.

Maybe I was mean. But if it's won me peace, it's worth it.

Paati's right. It's all a matter of how you deal with things.

And Chandra's right.

I'm strong. Even if my body is weaker.

My crutches tap out a victory march.

I strut,

tired but triumphant, toward school.

FIRST STEPS

"Is this my leg?"
A foot stuck on a metal pipe
all-too-visible through the transparent plastic "leg"
that doesn't match
the curve or the skin tone of my real leg.

"A trial limb. The clear plastic lets me check the fit.
You can practice with this
until the more modern one is ready."
Jim shows me a "silicone sleeve" that looks like a sock made of gel.
The sleeve fits over my residual limb.
A pin at the bottom of the sleeve
clicks to reassure me the leg is on properly
and clicks again when I take it off.
Jim's added soft straps above my knee for extra security.

"Ready to take the first step
toward your shining future?" Jim says.
Feeling as nervous as if I'm about to go onstage
for another dance competition,
I rise.

My body weight isn't even.
I'm leaning on my strong left side, stunned by the effort it takes
to raise my fake leg slightly off the floor.
How much strength did I lose
when they sawed off the muscles I once had?

My fake foot is cold, hard, senseless.
I glance down to see if it's correctly stationed.
I take another wavering step.
My brain can command my artificial leg, but plastic can't reply
like muscles and nerves can.
Hunched over, watching my hesitant feet
I shuffle like the beggar Paati and I met
on the way to the temple.

"Trust your sense of touch," Jim says.
"Walk like the dancer you are."
Circling around the room with him a second time,
I straighten up—back and neck erect.
It gets easier. My third round already
earns me Jim's usual compliment. "Great job!"
I wish I could vent my joy
by leaping.

"Start slow, kiddo. Wear this limb a few hours at first.
Build up slowly to an entire day.
Tell me what this limb does and doesn't let you do

so I can modify the design we have in mind. Okay?"
I suck in my cheeks to keep from sighing with impatience.

The next time we retrace our route, Jim says,
"Back home, my patients can hold a guard rail.
Here, though, I'm all the guard you've got."
I look at my hand tucked snugly in the crook of his elbow.
Sense the blond hair of his arm brushing against my skin.
Indian men don't invite ladies to hold on to their arms.
Feeling like the heroine of a Jane Austen novel
being courted by a British gentleman,
I giggle.
But my giddiness at being so near him
gives way to a spurt of anxiety when Jim says,
"Can you walk alone?
I need to see how your limb fits."
He lets go of my arm. "Trust my leg, kiddo.
Your leg, I mean."
"Our leg?" I suggest, surprising myself with my boldness.
Jim's eyes twinkle like the sea on a summer's day.
"As you wish, ma'am. Our leg."
His grin sends warmth rushing up my cheeks.

I move slow and unsteady around the room,
feeling the intensity
of his gaze
as it travels over every bit of exposed flesh.

Observes
my every movement.

Jim looks
preoccupied. Assessing.
I want him to look
admiringly. Appreciatively.
I want him to look at me
the way young men looked at me
that evening after my dance competition.

STUDYING
GRACE

"I'm going to study," I announce every evening.
Ma thinks I mean for my upcoming finals.
In my bedroom I study my reflection.
Attention focused on my feet.

After a million miles
a trillion minutes
walked with no thought at all,
I slow the motion down in my mind:
flex thigh, bend knee, lift ankle, straighten knee,
heel down, then the ball of my foot.
Bring my right foot down light enough
so it doesn't thud on the floor.
Lift high so it doesn't scrape or drag.
Match my left foot's pace precisely.

I must learn to walk gracefully first,
if I'm ever going to dance again.

BLUE
DIAMONDS

My fake leg well hidden under loose salwar trousers,
I walk to Chandra's housing development, three roads over.
Her ma wipes her moist eyes with the edge of her sari
when she sees me, saying,
"Can't believe you walked here. On your very own."
Chandra rushes over, followed by her pa and two older sisters.
The five of us chatter for a while,
just as we used to.
Her grandmother ambles over,
grumbles to me about her ailments.
I'm relieved
none of them treats me differently.

Chandra whisks me away for a private chat.
We sit on the back steps,
eating the spicy mixture of chickpeas, chili, and coconut
her mother cooked for us.

"Jim's so different from anyone we know," I tell Chandra.
"There's not one continent on earth he hasn't traveled to,
as far as I can tell,
and he knows all about making limbs and about physiotherapy,
which is pretty exceptional, I think,
but he never shows off."
Chandra raises her eyebrows. "You call your American doc
by name?"
"He's not exactly my doctor. It's like we're friends.
He even guesses my thoughts sometimes."
"So he's cute?"
"Not cute." Cartoon characters are cute. "He's . . . really manly.
Tall. Strong. He'd lift me out of the wheelchair easily,
no problem.
He's got brilliant blue-diamond eyes—"

"Not cute, only drop-dead gorgeous?" Chandra squeals.
"Youlikehim, youlikehim, youlikehim."
"Are you crazy?" I say. "He's probably thirty years old.
It's not like that.
Jim's really nice. That's all."
"Don't get mad." Chandra giggles. "I'm only teasing."

She pops a chickpea into her mouth. "Just be careful, okay?
My eldest sister's been dating a boy on the sly.
A rich boy and not even our same caste.
She said she was flirting for the fun of it,

to pass time until my parents arranged a husband for her.
Now she's gone and fallen in love with him.
You and your doc—it's a lot different, I know—but
he's attractive
and you're together a lot.
Don't lose your head over the wrong guy
like my sis."

CRUTCH FREE

Walking almost noiselessly,
free
of the clomp of crutches,
walking on my fake leg,
arms free to swing,
I feel as happy
as a pinioned bird whose wings are finally growing.

But every night, before taking off my limb for sleep,
I need to keep my crutches within arm's reach.
I'll never be completely
crutch-free.

NO *Longer* CENTER

Queuing up behind my classmates
the first day of exam week,
I realize no one's staring at me anymore.
Either because I blend in better without my noisy crutches
or because everyone's wrapped up in their own worries
about doing well.
A few of my classmates mutter prayers
as the doors of the long exam hall open.
"Good luck," Chandra and I wish each other.
Chandra's so anxious about exams her voice shakes,
though, as I tell her, I'm sure she'll excel.
The exam supervisor assigns me a seat
beneath a whirring ceiling fan that does little to ease the heat.
My residual limb itches with sweat.
I click my leg off under the desk,
read the question paper, scribble nonstop.
Three hours later, the exam supervisors announce,
"Drop your pens. Now."

Hungry for lunch, I spring halfway up on one leg,
forgetting the other's off.
Sway, clutch the desk to keep from falling,
sit down, and click my leg back on.

FAR
from the
ENVYING CIRCLE

Elated I'm nobody at school again,
eager to be somebody at dance class again,
I celebrate the end of exam week
by going to see my dance teacher
to prove to myself and to him
that I can keep on dancing.

"Shouldn't you wait for the better leg?" Paati asks.
I have waited
as patiently as a cactus waits for rain in the desert.
Jim will be pleasantly surprised when we meet next and I say,
"I'm dancing already."
He might even be so happy
he hugs me.

Uday anna's front door is open,
and when I enter,
Uday anna whips around.
"She's walking!" Kamini says.

"Come in. Sit down." Uday anna motions to a chair.
"We've missed you."

Missed me so much you didn't visit?
I don't ask.
Insulting him won't get me what I want.
I need to use my anger to fuel my dance.
"I've missed dance," I tell him. "But now I'm well
enough to start again."
"You've lost your leg!" He shakes his head
as though I've lost my mind.
"Sir, haven't you heard of Sudha Chandran?
She danced with an old-style Jaipur foot.
And I'm getting a far better prosthesis than hers. Soon."
"Veda, we must be practical—" Uday anna's reluctance
goads me on. I say,
"I
can
dance.
Even on *this* leg."

Feeling Kamini's eyes on me,
I turn to glare at her.
To my surprise, she shows me the symbol for friendship,
Keelaka hasta mudra:
the little fingers of her hands bent and locked together.
In her expression I see
no hint of envy.

She must be confident we'll never compete again.
Even the other girls stare at me
expectant,
not jealous.

I'll show them.
I assume the basic Bharatanatyam stance:
half-*mandi*.
Toes turned out sideways, heels slightly apart, I lower my hips,
bend my knees,
shape my legs into the sides of a diamond.
I raise my right foot, bring it down,
raise my left foot, bring it down.
Thaiya thai, thaiya thai. In slowest speed,
I can easily do
the first exercise every Bharatanatyam dancer learns.
Kamini says, "Very good." The girls clap.

"Veda?" Uday anna says. "You forgot to salute the earth."
Practice or performance, every Bharatanatyam dancer
must begin and end
every session by apologizing to the earth,
which dancers kick and stamp.
In my hurry to prove myself, I forgot to go through the motions.
"Sorry, Uday anna," I mumble, "I'll do it now."
My knees can bend enough to easily assume
the half-sitting posture.

I've never yet
forced them farther out—as far as they need to bend
for the full-sitting posture
the salutation requires.
What a fool I was not to test the limits of my flexibility
before I came.
Too late now.

I lower my torso, feet sideways, heels together.
I need to force my knees to bend out
with heels off the ground, balancing on tiptoe,
lowering my body down all the way
until my buttocks rest on my heels.
As I lower myself,
I lose my sense of center,
overbalance, tumble forward, and
crash-land on the ground.

"Veda!" Uday anna calls out. "Are you hurt?"
The girls cluster around me,
echoing Uday anna's concern.
Kamini helps me up.
"Thanks," I mutter.

I try once more.
Fall, almost, except Kamini catches me in time.
"No more," Uday anna says.

Kamini turns away
as though she can't bear to see me so clumsy.

Uday anna puts on his most gentle tone but
some words can't be softened.
"Veda, so many of us
blessed
with able bodies
can't meet the demands
of a professional dancer's life.
Maybe for you
it's time
for a new dream."

My body hurts from my falls
but Uday anna's words
hurt more.

UNEQUAL

Kamini follows me out of the classroom,
tears gushing down her cheeks
like a tap turned on full force.

I don't need anyone's pity.
"Don't feel so sorry for me, Kamini.
I'm still your equal.
Even with one leg less."

"No." Her lip trembles. "We aren't equal.
You're a better person."
"I'll be a better dancer again, too," I say.
She doesn't seem to hear me.
She's sobbing too loudly.
I hate how she's making a scene
out of my misery.
I'm the one who should be crying.

Still, it feels cruel to do nothing but watch
tears wrack her body.

I reach out and pat her back
until she stops shuddering.

Looking at me, she twiddles the free end of her dance sari.
After all these years of ignoring me
she seems to want to start a conversation
though she doesn't know how.

The skin under my leg hurts so much
I'm scared I'll start crying.

I wait for her to say something.
Until I'm too tired to control my tears any longer.
Hoping she can't see them rolling down my cheeks,
I hobble away
as fast as my pain lets me.

NOT BEST

I haul myself up the stairs of our apartment building,
nearly blind to Shobana's waving hand
nearly deaf to Mrs. Subramaniam's greetings.

Paati is asleep in her wicker chair, prayer book open on her lap.
Feeling older than Paati,
I walk into our room, take off my leg, towel my limb dry.
My smiley-mouth scar looks bright red
as though it's got lipstick on.
Chafed by my falls, the skin of my limb is raw.
I'll need to use crutches again until it's better.
Paati wakes up when I hobble back into the sitting room.
My voice hollow, I tell her,
"Uday anna doesn't want to teach me anymore."
Paati doesn't say I told you so,
you should have waited for the new leg.
Not that I'd expect her to.

She says something I expect even less.
"Good."
"Good?"

"Veda, that dance teacher of yours didn't visit your hospital
once.
He's not the only Bharatanatyam teacher.
Not even the best."

It's the first time I've heard Paati say something insulting
about another person.
I don't argue.

SACRED
Art
DEFILED

Paati lays a hand on my curls.
"Maybe you should see if Dr. Dhanam has a school."

"Dr. Dhanam?" Her name sounds vaguely familiar.
Paati has a faraway look in her eyes.
"Dr. Dhanam is a different kind of dancer.
Your *thatha* and I went to watch her once.
She focused on pure *abhinaya*—emotional expression.
A very unusual performance.
When she was done, the audience didn't clap.
Everyone was weeping. With joy.
It felt as though she'd given us a glimpse of heaven.
She danced only to devotional songs
expressing *Bhakthi rasa*, the love of God.
Onstage she became—invisible—"

"Invisible?" I'm not too sure what Paati means,
but maybe Dr. Dhanam

could teach me to improve my dance
in ways I've ignored.
If she doesn't turn me away.

"I'm not explaining well." Paati sighs. "How can I?
I never was a dancer."
The wistfulness in Paati's tone surprises me.
"Did you want to be a dancer, Paati?"
She never hinted at such a desire before.
Or maybe I wasn't listening.

"Dance was too much
for me to want.
It was forbidden to Brahmin girls like me.
Those days,
dance was practiced only by *devadasis*:
women who were supposed to dedicate their dances to God.
Bharatanatyam was meant to be a sacred art,
through which dancers could reach
a higher plane, carrying the audience with them.
They had a measure of freedom,
those women of the dancer caste.
Even wealth of their own.
But they paid a price, a terrible price.
They weren't allowed to marry.
And somehow, somewhere along the way,
society retracted

its promise to respect these women.
They were treated as prostitutes
and their sacred art degraded
into entertainment to please vile men."

NAILS
and
SPEARS

Thrust out of a nightmare
I wake to
pain.
Feel
nails and spears.
Jabbing.
Flesh throbbing beneath my knee
where nothingness should be.

My bladder is full.
I feel for my crutches.
Not by my bed
where they should be.

Clenching my teeth to keep from crying out,
I fumble for the light switch.
Paati's bed creaks as she shifts.
Her breathing sounds harsher than normal.
I mustn't wake her.

My frantic fingers
grope through the blackness
searching
for my crutches—or my leg.

At last I find
my leg under my bed.
A sputter of relief.
Tacking it on,
bladder almost bursting,
I hurl myself toward the bathroom.
Yank at the door.

My leg isn't
on properly.
I slip
on the cold tiles
of the bathroom floor.
Between my legs
a shameful trickle
I can't
control.

Lying in a yellow pool,
wetness seeping through my nightclothes,
I yank off the thing pretending to be my limb.
Shove it away
into the darkness.

I strip, clean myself, crawl,
find bleach and a sponge,
swab my mess off the tiles.
Naked. Wretched.

I notice Ma hovering—
holding my leg aloft
like a banner begging for truce.

How much of my degrading drama has she seen?
I fling words at her like shards of glass,
aiming to slash her apart.
"My accident was the answer to your prayers, wasn't it?
Happy I can't dance anymore?"

Ma lays the leg down beside me.
Cups my chin so I can't turn away.
Crouching,
she brushes the top of my forehead
with a kiss.

I don't remember the last time
Ma kissed me.
Long ago
maybe.
When I was a baby.

I'm too startled to pull away.

THE BEHOLDER

Jim's eyebrows shoot up in surprise
as I enter his office on crutches
and crumple into a chair.
"My dance teacher threw me out of his dance school."
"No way," Jim says.
His jaw clenches.
Then he bursts out, "What a fool.
What a poor excuse for a teacher.
You'll be an amazing dancer one day
and he'll regret his stupidity.
His loss, not yours, kiddo."

Hearing Jim's voice shake with anger
on my behalf,
I feel almost happy. I show him the red skin of my residual limb.
Jim whistles but he doesn't tell me how stupid I was.
I apologize. "I know I should've waited longer
but I tried dancing.
My knee wouldn't give enough.
It was so inflexible.
I fell when I tried full-*mandi*."

"You mean the pose in which
you lower your body all the way down
until you're sitting on your heels
with your legs folded under you
balancing on your toes with your knees to the sides?"

I nod, impressed at Jim's knowledge.
Hoping I don't sound whiny, I tell him,
"I can't dance without assuming that posture."
"Don't panic, kiddo. You know I've been reading up
on what your art demands of the body."
He waves at his bookshelf.
"You're giving me
just the kind of feedback I need
to adjust this trial limb.
And I'm going to make you a final prosthesis
that lets you sit cross-legged on the floor.
That's my challenge.
Your challenge is to
grind that fool's memory into the dust
under your dancing heels
and find a new dance teacher
who sees how special you are."

VISIONS

Jim saying I'm special
makes me feel brave enough to, with Chandra's help,
look up the dancer Paati admired—Dr. Dhanam.

"Great!" Chandra cries triumphantly.
She reads off the computer screen
a long list of Dr. Dhanam's accomplishments.
"Doctorate in classical dance, performed all over the world,
on the advisory board of practically every
Indian college dance program,
even some American universities.
Gave up performing years back.
Says she'll spend the rest of her life teaching.
Runs a dance school on her gorgeous home estate.
Perfect."
"Chandra, what if—if—she says no?"
"There's only one way to find out," Chandra says.

I look at the photograph of Dr. Dhanam.
Pointed chin, sharp nose,

arms triangulating over her head, elbows angled,
palms together.
All angles, corners, straight edges.
Except her eyes—
soft as velvety moss on a rock face.
Her face glows—ecstatic, blissful—
the way saints' faces must look
when granted
divine visions.

For the first time since the accident,
I hear the faint echo of a dancing rhythm.
Thaiya thai. Thaiya thai.

TO DANCE
AGAIN

Dr. Dhanam agrees to interview me
although I explain
I'm one-legged.
Hope coils inside me like a wound spring
as I walk up the shady drive that leads from the gate
past an open-air stage beneath a banyan tree
to a three-story mansion on her estate.
A maid shows me into a hall.
I sit waiting on the edge of an antique chair,
my foot tracing circles on the cold, hard floor.

Dr. Dhanam enters.
Her eyes take me in
without comment or pity.

Thank you, I think. "*Namaskaram*," I say,
pressing my palms together,
bowing my head low
in greeting, gratitude, and relief.

"Namaskaram, Veda. You may call me Dhanam akka.
You want to join my dance school? Why?"

"Ma'am—Dhanam akka—
I am—I mean I was—I mean I want to be
a dancer," I stammer.
"I started twelve years ago.
Performed onstage for a while.
Until I had an accident—
after I won a Bharatanatyam competition—"

"Bharatanatyam is not
about winning or losing," she interrupts.
"Competition distracts dancers
into thinking
this art is about them.
Art should be about something larger and deeper than self."

"But—didn't Shiva Himself compete at dance?
With His wife?"

Akka's thin eyebrows arch up.
She seems surprised I'm contradicting her. But also pleased.
She says, "Good to have a young one
stand up to me every now and then.
But you have forgotten, or perhaps not been taught,
the inner meaning of this parable.
The competition—between Shiva and His wife—

represents the longing
our limited human souls have
to understand and unite
with the divine soul."

Her tone is kind enough
but I feel foolish that I missed
knowing the deeper meaning of a story I performed.

"So, you want to relearn dance. But why come here, Veda?
Why not return to your old teacher?"
"He didn't want me back." I hope
I don't sound too angry at him.
"I see." She waits for me to say more.
Her silver toe-rings tap impatiently on the floor.
Thai thai. Thai thai.
The sound is a snatch of music, a dance rhythm,
carrying me back in time.
I see a little girl on her father's shoulders,
yearning to touch the feet of divine dancers
carved into temple walls.
I see her on a stepladder placing her hand on her chest,
feeling Shiva's dancing feet
in the beat of her heart.
"When I was little I felt my heart was beating
to the sound
of God's dancing feet.
Everywhere, in everything,

I could hear music to dance to.
When I grew up that music grew fainter
and I started to love applause.
I want someone who can help me feel dance
the way I used to.
I miss feeling dance inside me.
I miss hearing music in everything."

Akka gives me a sharp nod.
Encouraged, I continue. "My grandma said she saw
you dancing long ago.
That you treated dance as a sacred art,
an offering of devotion to God.
And I think I felt that way a little when I was young.
I want a teacher who can help me learn about that."

Akka's gaze pierces me. "Veda, if you want to relearn dance,
You'll need to begin at the beginning."
"Along with the little ones?"
Part of me cringes at the thought.
But I straighten up,
look her in the eye, and say, "Yes."

"As for fees, Veda, I do things the old way here.
Each student gives me whatever they can.
Some students pay nothing.
I leave it up to them
and their parents to decide what they can afford."

I'm her student already?
Without having to prove what I can or can't do physically?
And she doesn't care whether I pay?
It feels too good to be true. I stutter my thanks,
explain about the new limb I'll be getting soon.

Akka sets a date for my first lesson and says,
"Govinda, the student who teaches the beginners,
is about your age.
You'll learn from him until
you're ready to learn from me.
Come, I'll take you to him."

GREETING
GRACE

Dhanam akka leads me toward an airy classroom.
Pausing outside the door, I hear a sound I've missed:
the sound of feet raining a dance rhythm on the ground,
a sound that fills me with a desperate longing for dance
the way a wilting plant must long for water.

"Govinda!" akka calls.
A boy walks out of the classroom.
His body
long and muscular. Back perfectly straight.
A dancer's body.
His hair
a sheet of midnight. Sleek, shiny, shoulder length.
His eyes
pools of honey. Deep brown, flecked with gold.

"Govinda, this is Veda," akka says. "She was a dancer
but met with an accident
that cost her her right foot.

You'll be helping her relearn dance."
If Govinda feels shocked that he's getting a student who is a
below-knee amputee, he doesn't show it.
He presses his elegant, clove-dark hands together,
closes his eyes, and greets me the traditional way.
"Namaskaram."
His voice matches his looks—deep, rich, smooth.
The grace with which he bows his head and hands,
the seriousness with which he says Namaskaram,
as though he's chanting a prayer,
remind me of what the greeting means—
that he salutes the God within me.

When I return his greeting, pressing my palms together,
it feels magical instead of mechanical.

Govinda's gaze meets mine
and I burn with a desire to dance myself beautiful
in front of him.

A REAL
SMILE

"Dhanam akka's the one," I tell Paati
as I enter our apartment.
Breathing heavily, she heaves herself up
off the floor in front the household altar and says,
"Your teacher is lucky, Veda.
She's found a student who'll create a new world through dance
just as Shiva creates new universes through His steps.
A world where others with special limbs
will learn to enjoy their beauty."

First thing Pa asks after he and Ma come home,
"How was the new dance school, Veda?"
No surprise there.
What surprises me is how Ma reacts to my answer.
She smiles a real smile.

SEEING
BEAUTIFUL

In Jim's office,
I see a chair covered with a white sheet.
"Ta-da!" he cries as he whips it off,
revealing a nearly lifelike limb.
"Is your new limb to your liking, ma'am?"

My skin tone matches the limb's hue.
I stroke it. Something soft as flesh
fills the space between the metal skeleton and rubber skin.
I lift the limb.
It's lighter than my trial limb.
I try it on.
When they're side by side and compared closely,
my feet do look different. But no audience
could tell them apart if they saw me from a distance—onstage.
I press down on the toe.
When I ease off, I feel a springiness to the foot,
a push, giving me a faint pulse of energy back.
Almost a response.

"I love it!"

Jim grins. "Amazing, huh? That foot's durable, too.
Should last a couple of years. Won't wear out too quickly."
"Wear out?"
"Don't look so worried, kiddo.
The project will provide replacements.
Your foot will wear out
the way your shoes wear out.
No foot lasts a lifetime."

Except the ones we're born with.
Usually.

"Anything I can't do with this leg?"
I want him to say one word:
No.

Jim launches into a list.
". . . can't wear high heels . . .
. . . can tiptoe *only* if knees are bent . . .
. . . can't flex and point the foot . . .
but you'll be able to dance Bharatanatyam.
With this new leg
and faith in yourself
you can do pretty much anything
as far as I'm concerned.

"Now, ma'am, would you try out a few dance poses, please?
I want to make sure the fit's perfect."
Assuming the basic half-sitting pose
—feet splayed, knees out to the sides,
legs bent like the edges of a diamond—
I move my feet one at a time, slowly,
then at second speed,
then speeding up to third and fastest speed.

"Beautiful," Jim says.
My heart races.
The naked admiration in his voice
makes me feel grown up.
But then Jim
squats and taps
my unfeeling limb.
"Beautiful," he repeats. "Beautiful engineering,
beautiful design,
if I do say so myself."

BOULDER

Twice the age and size
of every other beginner in Govinda's classroom,
I feel as out of place as a boulder
brought down by the Ganga glacier
from the heights of the Himalayas
and abandoned on the river plain.

By the back wall of the sun-drenched classroom,
I skulk.
But I can't hide how I tower
over the rest of my classmates.

A little girl looks up at me. "You're so big!
Why're you in this class?"
While I wonder how to react,
Govinda states matter-of-factly
that I lost a leg in an accident,
that I have a new one I'm learning to dance with.
"But we're not here to chatter, children.
We're here to learn Bharatanatyam. Right?" he says.
"Right!" Their attention shifts back to him.

"We begin every dance session with a prayer," Govinda says.
Uday anna's class never began or ended with prayers.
"Aangikam bhuvanam yasya; Vaachikam sarvavaangmayam;
Aahaaryam Chandrathaaraadhi;
Tham Namah Saathvikam Shivam."
He who resides within every being in the universe;
who speaks the universal language;
whose ornaments are heavenly spheres;
Him we worship,
Shiva, the serene one.

Next, Govinda demonstrates
the dancer's apology to Mother Earth.
With ease,
the rest of the class imitates his movements.
Palms on the wall for support,
I manage to follow them,
my pose imperfect, but not too noticeably different.

We begin the first exercise, hands on hips,
knees bent, feet to the sides,
raising each foot off the ground and bringing it down,
thaiya thai, thaiya thai.

Govinda's voice fills the room.
"Empty yourselves of everything
except good thoughts."
My eyes fix themselves

on the feet rising and stamping the earth so effortlessly.
It's hard not to grudge the ease with which the others move.
I'm not sure I can empty myself of wishing
for those able bodies I don't own.

TOUCH
LOST

Pa, Ma, Paati, Chandra, all ask,
"How does the new leg
feel?"

I don't point out
their question misses a point:
Even this new leg
doesn't
feel.
I won't ever feel
five of my toes,
my ankle,
my instep,
my heel.
My right foot will never tell me if the floor is
wet/dry,
hot/cold,
flat/sloping,
rough/smooth,
bumpy/slippery.

My right leg has
lost touch with the world.

But when they ask,
I say,
"Amazing,"
because it feels amazingly better than the old trial limb
and because I know
that's the answer
they need to hear.

ONLY
Three
TALENTS

Tired of holding the wall
when I perform the apology to the Earth Goddess,
I try it without support
although a tremor crawls up my spine
at the thought of falling in front of the children.
My feet and knees to the sides, I lower my torso,
my back erect.
I feel the weight on my left side rolling onto the ball of my foot,
feel my left heel lift off the ground.
But I can't sense what my right foot is doing.
Unbalanced,
I tumble out of position.
My bottom bumps on the ground.

A giggle erupts and spreads.
The entire earth seems to shake with scorn.
I am a fallen piece of rubble.

"Silence." Govinda's eyes
leap like angry flames.
Every trace of laughter dies.
Govinda instructs the class to continue,
walks over to face me and assumes the pose himself:
knees bent all the way to the sides,
resting his torso on his heels, legs folded in half beneath him,
balancing on tiptoe, back perfectly straight.
He's so close I catch the faint coconut scent of his hair.
"Veda, our ancient scriptures say
the best dancers must have ten talents:
balance,
agility,
steadiness,
grace,
intelligence,
dedication,
hard work,
the ability to sing well,
to speak well,
and to see deeply and expressively.
You've only lost the first three talents.
Only for a while."

The three I need most.
What use are the rest?

"Soon you'll regain all ten talents."
Govinda waits.
In the depths of his eyes I see no pity.
Only patience and trust.
His hands stretch on either side of my waist
between the edge of my blouse and the top of my skirt
near enough to hold me from another fall
but not touching.
He thinks I can do it on my own.
"Only three have you lost.
Only temporarily.
You have all seven other talents."
He repeats those words
as though they're an incantation.

Listening to his resonant voice,
I rise to my mismatched feet.

TWO MEN

Our exam results arrive.
Chandra tops the list.

Paati and my parents sign a card for her and
Chandra and I go to her favorite café—Java Joy—to celebrate.
"Your family must be thrilled," I tell her. "My ma's backed off
since the accident,
but deep down
she probably still wishes I could be an engineer.
She'd exchange you
for me
any day."

Chandra stabs a piece of cake. "Your family gives me
so much attention.
Mine hardly notices my achievements.
Everything I do, one of my sisters did already.
Plus, you know that boy my sister was seeing in secret?
His parents found out about them.
They were angry because they're wealthier and a different caste.

So he dumped her.
She's miserable, poor thing.
She was so upset she even told my parents about him
after they broke up.
So my parents are in a tizzy trying to set her up
with a suitable boy now. No time for me."
To steer Chandra's thoughts away from her family,
I ask if she's decided what she wants to do in college yet,
though college is still years and many exams away.

"I'm going to become a biomedical engineer,"
she says, starting to cheer up. "Someday
I'll make a leg that'll listen to your brain
so you can do every Bharatanatyam pose you can think of."
I'm glad my accident at least helped
Chandra figure out her career path.

Chandra spears another piece of cake.
"Speaking of dance poses, how's it going with dancer boy?
He sounds interest-ing. And interest-ed."

No boy is going to find me
attractive.
Least of all someone as gorgeous as Govinda.

"He's helping you out *a lot*," Chandra says.
I shrug. "He's helping me out. Yes. Not asking me out."

"Do you like him better than Jim?" Chandra asks.

I roll my eyes. "I don't *like* either of them that way."

But her question makes me uncomfortable.

In my mind, I see Jim and Govinda side by side.

Govinda standing tall like the dancer he is,

beautiful, serious, and as deeply in love with dance as I am;

Jim with his hands in his pockets, a teasing look in his eyes,

a cheerful glow lighting his face.

Jim, who's traveled the world and still finds me special.

Chandra sings, "Veda's in love with two men.

Who's she going to pick?

Veda's in love with two men. With whom will she stick?"

I ball up a tissue and toss it at her face.

BOLDER

"Look at you walk,"
Jim says. "Can hardly tell you're wearing a prosthesis.
I'm so proud of you.
How's the dance coming?"

"I love the spring in my new foot and
how much flexibility this leg gives my knee.
But I still can't do the full-sitting pose easily."
I sink as low as I can, knees out sideways,
legs almost folded in two,
showing him how hard it is to keep my balance.
Then I assume the lunge position:
one leg straight back, toes on the ground,
the other forward, bent at the knee,
torso straight.
"Can't leap into this lunge position the way I'm supposed to.
Can't do any exercise involving it without falling."

"Not yet," Jim says. "Does the leg pinch? Rub your skin sore?"
"No, but I tire too easily."
"Veda, you'll build up stamina. Faster than you think."

Jim shows me squats to strengthen my left leg.
Exercises to help me work toward the poses I find difficult.

We spend more time together than usual.
He looks up at the clock and whistles.
"We need to stop, kiddo."

Jim runs his rough fingers through his hair
and stares at his poster-filled wall.
His eyes dim.
He looks lonely.
Lost and lonely, like a stray puppy on the street.
Not the easygoing Jim who jokes with me.

"Something wrong?" I wish I could help him.
Wish I could be part of his life outside this room
as a true friend would be.

"Just feeling a bit blue, kiddo.
I need to make some big decisions soon."

I blabber, "Maybe you need a cup of coffee? And some cake?
There's a nice café quite nearby—Java Joy.
Going there usually cheers up my friend Chandra."

"Good idea. Maybe I'll go there later.
Enjoy that leg until we meet again, okay?"
He turns to his computer.

I wasn't recommending he go there on his own.
Didn't he realize I was inviting him to go there
with me?
I take a deep breath.
Jim stops typing
and looks up, startled,
as though he's wondering
why I'm still standing around.
"Another question I can help with, kiddo?"

"I was trying—wanted to say—I wish—you—I
hope that decision thing doesn't get you down."
I flee
as fast as my new leg will let me.

SYMMETRY

"Today, you'll be moving your hands
instead of keeping them at your waist," Govinda says.
The class twitters with excitement.

Govinda beckons to me.
"Please come up front?
I need your help."
He stands so close behind,
I can almost feel his long fingers
touching my back.

"Watch how Veda holds her head and her neck
so it lengthens her spine.
I want you to stand just the way she does.
Imagine a line passing from the center of your head,
through your navel, down to your feet.
Every movement should begin along this line and return to it.
Hold your arms as evenly as Veda.
See the perfect symmetry
with which her right hand mirrors her left?"

The lilting notes of a bamboo flute
play a melody in my mind.

The remaining class time
flies.

A TIME
to
SPEAK

First day of school after the summer holidays,
I pretend Govinda's standing behind me
speaking about my perfect stance
as Chandra and I walk toward school.
Inside the building, we part ways for the first time.
She hurries off to join
the science-math-computer-engineering classes.
I walk toward the history-literature-language section
that's dominated by girls and boys who haven't got good grades
or much ambition.

In my new classroom, I see Mekha and Meghna.
The twins' long-ago insults ring in my ears.
Should we start calling cricket stumps something else
because she has a stump?
"Look who's here!" Mekha calls out. "Veda!
Hey, Veda, does my hair look *limp* today?"
Meghna sniggers.

I think of the little kids in my dance class
who didn't know any better
laughing the first time they saw me fall.
Mekha and Meghna aren't innocent.
They're nasty girls
who should know better.

The rest of the class is quiet—
waiting to see what I'll do.

"Some stupid people are
smart enough to hide their stupidity," I say.
A twitter runs through the class. My classmates are laughing.
At Mekha and Meghna.

I stride past the twins
as if they don't exist.

NOT ENOUGH

Jim gives me a long, serious look
when I next see him.
"Remember what I said
about having to make some big decisions?
The decision impacts you."
My heart pirouettes.
"I've decided," he says,
"to return to America."
I bite my lip so hard it hurts.

"But don't you worry.
I'll be leaving you in good hands."
Not
the hands I want.

"I'll miss you," he says,
"but every project comes to an end, you know."
I *should* have known.

I can't believe I was stupid enough
to think he cared for me.
That I was special to him.
"You'll do great, kiddo."
"I'm not a kid," I mutter.
"I know. I know." He pats the top of my head
as if he's pacifying a baby. "You're one special young woman."

"Not special enough for you," I blurt.
Jim looks as though an earthquake just struck. "What?"

Awkwardness
hangs
in the space
between us.

I wish the earth would spin backward,
erase the last minute and those words
I never meant to say to his face.
"Veda—I'm sorry if—if anything I said or did made you
think—"
I shake my head. It was all me.
My mistake.
I read too much into everything.
Dreamed, imagined, and
let my thoughts get
as out of control as my body.

"Veda," he says. His tone is kind, patient, gentle.
"It's normal to get attached to your caregiver.
You'll get over it soon."

I sense he's trying to make me feel better,
though it only makes things worse
to hear Jim say I'm as ordinary
as any other patient.

"We'll meet before I leave. Okay, Veda?"
His forehead crinkles with concern.

Feeling more like a kid than when he called me kiddo,
I nod my head and
walk out the door he holds open.

BARE

The words *not special enough for you* ring in my ears
louder and clearer than when I actually blurted them to Jim.
My foolish words even interrupt my sleep,
waking me in the early dawn.

Paati will be up soon.
But this problem she can't help with.
She wasn't allowed to think about boys or men.
Except the one her parents arranged for her to marry.
She couldn't possibly understand
how stupid and confused I feel.

I get my leg on and pace
up and down our balcony.
"Veda?" Ma's *potu*
is a smudged red blur on her forehead.
She rubs a bare earlobe with her thumb.

"Ma? Why aren't you wearing your earrings?"
Ma looks at me with sleep-dimmed eyes.

Dr. Murali said Jim's project would subsidize the cost,
not cover everything.
I never bothered to think how much my medical bills cost
or where the money to pay them would come from.
"Ma? You sold your diamonds to pay
my bills?"

"When we named you Veda," Ma says,
"I remembered the four holy books called the Vedas.
I'd forgotten that dance is also called the fifth Veda.
Until after the accident, I didn't want to accept
you'd chosen that fifth Veda
over any book.
But I should have known
when you and I argued about dance
and I saw your jaw set in the same stubborn line
as mine when I argued with my parents
for permission to marry your pa.
My family wanted me to marry a richer man
so I'd have the security of wealth.
I gave up wealth so I could have this family.
Yet I wanted you to have a well-paid career
that would bring you the comforts I'd once had."

Ma shakes her head at herself.
"I imagined you'd wear my earrings
on your wedding day.

But that was silly.
Even I didn't marry wearing my ma's jewelry.
So, yes, I sold my earrings to pay
our bills."
Ma reaches for my hand.
Our fingers interlock.
Between us,
shadows shorten and lighten
as the sun creeps higher into the sky.

"For your sake," Ma says,
"I'd have begged my family for money
if I had no earrings to sell.
Your future matters more than my pride.
After all, you're my most precious jewel, Veda."

EXCHANGES

Govinda walks me out of class.
"Akka asked how you were doing.
I said you're doing so well
we need to start working one-on-one."

We. Govinda said we.
And he not only thinks of me outside class,
he wants to give me private lessons!
"But—" I hesitate. "It would take up so much of your time."

"I learn when I teach.
You'd be doing me a favor."
He looks sincere.
"Or am I not a good enough teacher?"
He sounds hurt.

"You're an amazing teacher!
The best."

In the dark pools of Govinda's eyes
gold flecks shimmer like fish scales. "Is that a yes?"

I stop short,
feeling suddenly shy. "Yes."

"Akka has a carpeted study
she sometimes lets older students use.
If we met there, we wouldn't have to worry
about you falling on a hard floor.
I'll ask her if we can use it
and call to schedule a lesson, okay?"

Govinda actually worries about me hurting myself.
I wish my leg would let me twirl with joy.

"Your parents don't have a problem with boys calling,
do they?"

"No," I say, though I don't actually know.
I've never given a boy my number before.
He couldn't like me.
Could he?

A PARTIAL
VICTORY

Alone in akka's carpeted study with me, Govinda chants aloud,
"Thath thai thaam, dhith thai thaam,"
and I try to lunge,
lurch like a drunkard but manage to hold my ground.

"Almost!" Govinda says.
I stamp my foot in frustration.
"Almost means nothing.
A partial victory is a complete defeat."

"Are you dancing or fighting a war?"
Govinda gives me one of his rare smiles.

If he's trying to be funny, he's failing.
"I'm used to winning over my body.
Now I'm always losing to it."

My tone wipes the grin off Govinda's face.
"Dance isn't about winning or losing," he says,

"it's about enjoying how your body moves."

I kick my right leg out so ferociously I almost lose balance.
"This
isn't
my
body."

"We all choreograph to our strengths, Veda.
The audience won't see
what you don't show them."

"I don't want to be a good
handicapped
dancer.
I want to be a good dancer," I shout.

"You think akka's body has no
limitations?" Govinda shouts back.
"You think because she's older and less flexible
she's not as good a dancer anymore?
Being a good dancer is more
than mastering
every pose there is."

"We're not talking about every pose there is.
Because of my leg, some poses are off limits.

Entirely.
So I must master
everything else that's possible.
Can't you see that?"

"Some dancers thrill audiences
with exotic poses and excessive speed.
I think you should
care more about entering people's hearts
and elevating their souls
than about entertaining their minds.
I think you should start
getting over your obsession with what you can or can't
do physically.
Bharatanatyam dance is not just
about perfecting your body's skills."
Govinda sits down and taps out the rhythm
using his block and stick.

Govinda's words
wound me more deeply
than when Kamini
said my dance wasn't spiritual enough
after I won the competition.

We don't speak for the rest of the hour.
I try twisting in the full-sitting pose and leaping into a lunge,

try and fail,
fail many times,
fail spectacularly.

My only accomplishment, when I leave class:
I've fought so hard with Govinda,
I've had no time to think of being embarrassed about Jim.

AS MANY
Perfect Poses
AS PEOPLE

"Govinda doesn't understand me!" I complain to Paati.
"He wants me to skip every pose that's hard
instead of helping me perfect them.
He wants me to skirt hurdles, not leap over them."

In answer, Paati tells me a story.
"The sage Vyasa once climbed
the snowy peaks of the Himalayas,
where Shiva lives.
Eager to perfect every yoga pose, Vyasa asked Him,
'How many yoga asanas are there?
I wish to master every pose so I can be the best yogi of all time.'
Shiva replied,
'There are as many perfect poses as there are people.'
And Vyasa understood that yoga
is about embracing the uniqueness within.
Shiva sees perfection in every sincere effort.
He loves us despite—or maybe because of—
our differences."

ONLY
Temporarily
ABLE

At the Java Joy café, Chandra jabs her spoon at me.

"How are your private dance lessons going?

Have you been flirting with your dance-teacher boy?"

I choke, scorching the roof of my mouth.

Chandra pats my back until I stop spluttering.

"Flirt? Me? I'm useless with guys.

I blurt out idiotic things in front of them.

Or get angry and push them away."

"You and Govinda fought?

About what?"

"Govinda insisted everyone has limits

and even able-bodied dancers get old and inflexible.

I got mad

because I'm young and inflexible."

Telling Chandra what Govinda said,

I realize he wasn't being unreasonable.

On the TV screen, I see Shastri, whom Ma and Pa said

was the "baby" of the national cricket team

when they were young.

Now he's an old man sitting in the commentator's box.

"Call him and apologize," Chandra advises.

"It must be hard for you to relearn dance, Veda,

but it's not his fault.

Don't fight with him. Flirt with him."

"He's too serious to flirt with, Chandra."

"Too serious? Who do you think you are? Ms. Frivolity?"

Chandra lifts another spoonful of froth.

I watch the bubbles burst like weak excuses.

"But the new leg is good?" Chandra asks. "Jim is helping?"

I swirl my teacup so fast, chai slops on the table.

"Chandra, I was so stupid.

I—I—I went and told Jim that I liked *him*."

Chandra laughs. "Nice try, Veda. I almost believed you."

She starts mopping up the spilled chai.

Her disbelief makes me feel worse.

"I'm not kidding, Chandra.

Jim was shocked at first. Then really nice about it.

So nothing creepy happened.

I just feel foolish."

Chandra gapes.

Finally, she says, "I'm sorry.

That was crazy but it took guts.

More guts than most of us have."

She hugs me. "It'll be okay.

Maybe it's even a good thing you said it.

Gets it off your chest.

Jim was cricket practice; Govinda's the real match.

Match. Get it?"

She looks so pleased with her pun,

she makes me smile.

REACHING
OUT

At home, I dial Govinda's number.

Hang up after two rings.

Silly, silly. I'm not calling to ask him out.

I rehearse my speech:

Govinda, this is Veda. I'm sorry I shouted at you.

I dial and don't hang up. A woman's voice answers.

I assume it's his mother, then realize it's the maid

because she calls me "ma'am"

and I hear her in the background

addressing Govinda with respect: "Govinda, sir."

"Hello?" His voice is just as musical on the phone

as it is face-to-face.

"Govinda, this is Veda. I'm sorry I shouted at you."

"That's okay."

"See you in class tomorrow?"

"Sure." It's a short word.

Too short for me to tell if he's pleased or not.

"Thanks."

"Sure."

Later I wonder
what it's like to be rich and have a live-in maid
who answers the phone.
I ask Ma if it was hard to give up
her wealthy way of life when she married Pa.
"Giving up money wasn't hard," Ma says.
"But though I was never very close to my
parents or siblings,
it was hard that they cut off contact altogether.
Still is."

A SENSE
of
NORMAL

Jim invites Ma and Pa to come with me
to meet one last time at his office
and go to his farewell party.

"Hello, kiddo." Jim looks
as friendly as when we first met.
No awkwardness at all.
The gratitude I feel toward him deepens.

He introduces me and Pa and Ma
to the kind-eyed Indian lady who'll be taking over his "cases,"
though he says, "You're doing so great, kiddo,
you'll only need to see her for a few checkups
until you've worn out your leg."
Then he walks us over to a large hall
filled with his other patients
who've gathered to say good-bye.

I meet a girl who says she kicks the soccer ball
better with Jim's leg than her own.
A middle-aged woman makes me laugh
as she expounds the virtues of being one-legged:
"Cuts pedicure bills in half."

At this party, celebrating the legs Jim will leave behind,
two-legged people are in the minority.
We amputees are the norm.

Jim says, "When you're on your first
dance tour in America, kiddo,
call me. I'll be in the front row."

My throat feels
as rough as his hands
which hold mine
for what might be the last time in this life.
"Thanks, Jim.
For everything."

FEAR
of
FALLING

When I see Govinda, he says, "Sorry we fought.
I agree you need to try and master
whatever your leg doesn't prevent you from doing.
But I hope someday you'll learn to move
the mind and heart, not just your body."

We pick up where we left off:
try to balance in the full-sit,
try to lunge without stumbling.

On the ground after my thirteenth fall of the day,
I pummel the carpet in frustration.
"You look like my kid sister
throwing a temper tantrum," Govinda says.
Being Govinda's kid sister is almost as bad
as being Jim's "kiddo."

"Veda? We're going to play a game."
Now Govinda's acting as if I am his kid sister.

"I'm
not
a
kid."
Or his sister, but I don't add that.

"I'm
your
teacher." Govinda mimics my voice.
"Listen to me for once."
He walks to a far corner of the study,
sits in the chair by the writing desk,
stretches his long legs out, and says, "Stand on my feet."

"Stand on your feet?"
"Place your feet sideways over mine, Veda.
Toes on the floor. Knees bent in the half-sitting pose."
"Why?"
"Please?"

I position myself the way he wants,
my toes touching the earth,
my feet crisscrossing over his,
my knees bent out to the sides.
He stretches out his hands and tells me to lay my palms on his.

We're touching.
The entire length of both my palms

on both of his.
Music fills my ears—fast, high-pitched,
like the buzz of a bee.
We're closer than I've been to any other boy my age.
And Govinda looks gorgeous,
loves dance,
and is an amazing, generous teacher.
He lifts
his legs,
his feet,
and me
into the air.
I shriek like a delighted child.

Govinda recites the words of a child's game:
"Mamarathilla yerade, mangaye parikade."
Don't climb the mango tree, don't pluck the mango fruit.
I played this game with Pa, when I was little,
my tiny feet planted entirely on his,
his legs lifting me as high as they could,
bouncing me up and down.
I'd feel like I was flying.
Govinda isn't lifting me nearly as high as Pa did,
isn't keeping me in the air as long,
but I'm older and heavier.
He must be so strong
to bear my weight.

"Want you to enjoy
feeling your body move," Govinda says,
"thought it might help your sense of balance, too."

"Again?" I feel my face flush
with childish excitement.
Govinda grins. "I thought you weren't a kid?"
I push my lips into an exaggerated pout.
We laugh and he lifts me once more.
His muscles tighten with strain.

I shift from side to side,
stretch,
rock,
reorient my body to my new sense of balance.
Give in to the thrill of almost-falling,
secure in the shelter of Govinda's arms.

DEMONS

I stand up after falling from my lunge—
and say, "Again."

Govinda shakes his head. "You dance like a demon, Veda."
Is he starting another fight?
But he says, earnestly, "It's a compliment."

"If that's a compliment," I say,
"I'd hate to hear your insults."
"Your strength, and only your strength,"
Govinda clarifies, looking worried,
"reminds me of the demon
whom Shiva fought,
the demon whose strength doubled
whenever he fell to the ground."

"You have to work a lot harder
on your compliments."
"You inspire me to work harder," he says,
"on a lot of things."

"Such as what?"

"Such as my life. What I want to accomplish,"

Govinda explains. "My parents are engineers.

They want me to take over their engineering firm.

They don't understand

how much I love teaching dance.

How little I care about making money."

"My ma was that way," I say. "Focused on me being an engineer.

Until my accident, we fought a lot.

Don't know how it would have gone

if I hadn't lost my leg."

"I know how it would have gone.

You'd have forced your ma to come around.

You have no trouble fighting for what you love.

I'm not a fighter like you are, Veda,

but I'm hoping some of your spirit will rub off on me."

So Govinda does admire me.

Thath thai thaam, dith thai thaam.

I kick, sink down into full-*mandi*, lunge,

and leap up.

And land in the standing position.

"Yes! Yes! Yes!" Govinda punches the air.

I stand with both feet flat and sure on the floor,

prepared to try some more,

but Govinda says, "Maybe we should end with that today?
You know we've started working
on a dance drama about the Buddha's life
and I'm playing the lead?
Akka wanted to start rehearsing earlier today."
"Can I come watch?" I ask.
"I don't dare say no to my demon." Govinda's tone is
affectionate.
And half teasing.
His demon?
This is the first time Govinda's ever called me "his."
My heart skips.

But maybe I'm making too much out of what Govinda said.
Maybe a nickname means
no more to Govinda than it did to Jim.

A NEW CENTER

Govinda and I walk
toward the open-air stage beneath the banyan tree
where the cast is assembled.

Dhanam akka arrives.
She says a small problem has come up.
There's a role vacant in the play.
A student—Renuka—is moving away.

"Tough role," someone comments.
"Wasn't Renuka playing the old, sick woman Buddha sees
who's onstage for three whole minutes?"
Laughter ripples through the rest of the cast.
I say, "Please may I have that part?"

Everyone's gaze shifts to me.
On Govinda's face, I catch a look of admiration.
I say, "If I keel over, it'll only add a touch of realism."

"You may have that part, Veda.
And the part of Gautami," Dhanam akka adds.

Govinda looks puzzled. "Gautami?"
"We'll add a short scene to the play,"
akka says. "The story of Gautami.
Veda will play her role as well."

A little girl runs up to us.
"This is my kid sister, Leela," Govinda says.
"I'm not a kid," Leela says,
hands on hips. "I'm eight and a half."
"Namaskaram," I say, as seriously as I'd greet any adult.
"It's very nice to meet you, Leela."
The entire cast surrounds us.
A pretty girl who looks my age, though a lot shorter,
with dimpled cheeks and large eyes,
extends her hand in friendship.
"I'm Radhika," she says. "Govinda's neighbor."
After years of being envied at my old dance class,
after weeks of being whispered about at my school,
I'm encircled
by welcoming smiles.

JUST AS WARM

When I tell them I'll be onstage soon
(although with many others, playing just two tiny roles),
Chandra whoops,
Paati wraps me in her plush arms,
Pa lifts me a foot off the ground,
and
Ma
gives me a hug.
Not nearly as soft as Paati's
but just as warm.

NOT EVEN
an
OLD WOMAN

My first part in the play should be easy.

All I have to do is hobble onstage with a cane.

But I don't even play an old woman well enough

to please Dhanam akka.

"Buddha was born a prince," she says. "It was prophesied

He could rule the whole world.

Yet when He saw your plight,

He gave up His entire kingdom,

His wealth, His power,

His family.

You made Him yearn to seek a way

to end all human suffering.

Your role in the play represents the pain of all humanity.

The sight of you—poverty-stricken,

overcome by age and illness—

turned Buddha from a mere man

into a reincarnation of God."

According to Paati's story there were
four sights that moved Buddha:
one old person, one afflicted with illness, a corpse,
a monk whose face glowed peace.
But I don't correct akka.

My second role is even harder.
In my second role, I am Gautami,
a woman who came to the Buddha
with her dead son in her arms,
begging Him to bring her son back to life.
Wiping the tears from her cheeks, Buddha asked her
to bring Him a mustard seed from the home
of a family that had never suffered.
Gautami left her son's body at His feet
and went from house to house,
searching for a family that had not known pain.
No family could give her a mustard seed
because every family had seen sorrow.
Instead, they gave her comfort and shared tales of loss.
Speaking and listening to stranger after suffering stranger,
Gautami saw that death came to everyone
and she accepted the tragedy that had struck her life.
Returning to where her son's body rested,
she felt embraced by the compassion in His eyes.
Knowing that her son's soul lived on,
Gautami cremated her son's body.

To play Gautami's role, I must show
not only pain but also acceptance and peace.

After rehearsal,
Radhika, who plays the Buddha's kind stepmother,
pulls me aside.
"Akka's hard on all of us
during rehearsals.
Once, she yelled at me ten minutes straight," she says.
Radhika is sweet to try comforting me.
But though I sincerely thank her,
I still feel frustrated at myself
as I trudge down the drive.

Govinda catches up with me.
"Veda, are you all right?"
"I don't know what akka wants of me.
I can't tell what I'm doing wrong."
"Akka thinks of dance as a way to help our souls progress
through our many incarnations.
She wants us to use dance to engage
with our deepest emotions,
not to escape ourselves and the world.
She says we can learn
about Karma and acting rightly in this life
through the characters we become in a dance-drama."

Govinda's feet keep pace with my mismatched pair
all the way to the bus stop.
More than his words, I'm comforted by the sight
of his feet, waiting alongside mine,
until my bus arrives.

THE PAIN
of
LOSING
⚮

At home, I find Paati in her wicker chair, rubbing her temples,
looking as though she has a headache.
I fetch the sesame oil to massage away her pains,
the way she'd do mine.
"Akka says I need to show the pain of humanity better,
though I'm only onstage for a few minutes in the first role.
And she cast me as Gautami—I don't know why,
given she isn't pleased
with how I play the first role."
Paati says, "Losing someone you love
probably isn't so different from losing a part of your body.
I doubt many other students
know pain as well as you do."

THE THIRD EYE

Dhanam akka says she
wants me to work on my part.
With her. Alone.
Akka leads me to the hall where we first met
and motions me to a chair.
She touches the red dot at the center of her forehead.
"Veda, do you know why we wear a potu?"
Her tone is gentle.
And the last thing I expected
was for her to ask me a question.
I'm too surprised to answer.

"The dot symbolizes your third eye," she says.
"We wear it to remind ourselves
to look with knowledge and compassion,
as a true guru would.
When we use our inner eye,
we see with our minds and our hearts.
We see truth; we see beauty; we see Shiva.
Inside you, Veda, I sense the flame of extraordinary courage,
but not enough compassion.

If you must dance, the way I want my students to,
you must learn to be compassionate.
To yourself
and to others.
Acknowledge your pain.
Allow yourself to feel your loss."

I don't mind pushing my body to test my balance.
I don't want to push my mind
back into that cold pit where the accident led me.
But if that's what it takes to dance again,
I'll make myself relive
the tree coming closer
the smells of burnt rubber, of vomit, of blood.
Screaming
silence.

Shivering, almost doubled over, I take a step
down into the space where light is an enemy
but not even darkness shrouds my terror.
Another step
into hospital corridors
winding like snakes.
I enter my writhing mass of fear, horror, desperation.
And stay there.
Tears streak down my cheeks.
Seen through tears my new foot seems softer,
my five stiff toes blurred at the edges.

Akka stretches her arms out toward me.

And I realize

she's showing me I'm strong enough to reenter the pit of despair

because she wants to help me

climb all the way out.

DRAGONS
and
GECKOS

Govinda is waiting for me
on the empty stage under the banyan tree.
He asks, "How did your session with akka go?"
"Draining and strengthening. Both.
Thanks for waiting for me, but I know it's late, Govinda.
I understand if you don't have time to work with me today."
"You understand?" His voice
sounds as rich and deep when he teases
as it does when he's serious. "Miracles do happen.
My demon is softening. She's understanding."
"I thought I was your little sister. Not your demon."

Govinda doesn't clarify where I stand in his affections.
He grins and waves a gift-wrapped package in front of my face.
"For you."
"Why? It's not my birthday or anything." I reach for it.
Govinda snatches it away just as my fingers touch the ribbon.
"It's not your birthday or anything?
Maybe I should wait and give it to you later."

"Give it here." I dart forward.

"Come and get it," he taunts, quickening his pace,

keeping the package just out of my reach.

He makes me chase him,

then lets me pin him against the banyan's trunk.

"I got you to run fast.

That, in itself, should count as a lesson," he says,

raising the package high above his head.

We tussle for it. A button on his shirt pops

and I feel the bare skin of my waist

press against his skin.

The package feels hotter than a handful of flames.

I let go.

Govinda hands it to me.

I untie the ribbon and open the package.

Inside is a bright yellow paper kite

in the shape of some four-legged animal with a long tail.

"Like it? I made it."

I love how uncertain he looks.

And most of all

that he spent time and effort to make me something.

"It's beautiful, Govinda. Is it a

. . . gecko?"

He groans. "My sister thought it was, too.

It's meant to be a dragon."

"Geckos are sort of like real-life dragons.
Kind of magical, you know?
They have the power to regrow lost tails."
My words surprise me but it's good to find
I'm no longer envious of animals
whose powers of regeneration I lack.
"I don't know how to fly kites, though."

"If there's a field near your place and your parents don't mind,
I could come by and teach you," he offers.
He's so focused on me,
I feel I can see his soul shining
in the depths of his eyes.

FLIGHT
of
FEELING

I'm in the bedroom
trying to choose the prettiest dot to wear on my forehead
when I hear Pa welcome Govinda in.
My heart thuds
as though I'm dancing in the third and fastest speed.

Govinda's voice is offset by a high-pitched childish one.
He's brought his sister along.
I try not to feel too disappointed.
We will still have time together,
he did make me a gift for no reason,
and bringing her shows how nice he is to everyone.

Mrs. Subramaniam's eyes pop out of their sockets
when she sees me and Govinda
walking out of our building together.
I realize I've never seen Shobana
or even any of her older daughters with a boy.
Until they were engaged.

When we reach the field,
Govinda whispers, "Sorry I brought Leela.
I have a hard time saying no to her."

"You're a sweet older brother.
Nothing wrong with that," I say.

A caged look comes over Govinda's face.
"I'm still having a hard time saying no
to what my parents want me to do with my life, too, though.
I hate disturbing the peace and that's not always good."

I try to lighten his mood.
"You'd prefer to be a demon like me?"

"I actually would." He touches my chin with a forefinger.
"I'd love to be brave enough, clear enough,
to show them how much I want to be a dancer.
Every time the topic comes up, my pa and ma tell me
how hard they've worked
so I could have a comfortable life,
how long it took to establish their firm and make it flourish,
how it's my duty to earn well
so I can look after them in their old age
and my duty to look after their legacy that I'll inherit."

"Maybe you should try having an accident.
Worked well with me and my ma."

Shaking his head, Govinda smiles.
"Can't believe you can joke about that!"

Leela interrupts us,
yanking at Govinda's arm and yelling, "Help me fly my kite!"
He ruffles her hair.
Leela shrieks, "I'm flying, I'm flying,"
as they launch her kite into the clear sky.

It's my turn next.
"Keep the string taut." Govinda shouts instructions at me.
I feel a gust of air catch my kite, lift it, then suddenly drop away,
almost sending it crashing into the trees.
I reel the line in.
The yellow paper tail loops, swirls,
climbs until it's a tiny golden streak,
long tail glittering.
I take tiny steps, forward and back.
The sun warms my face and I feel the wind racing
as if my kite is carrying me into the sky.
I feel small. Light.
Hear a tinkling tune in my ears—high and sweet—
the sound of silver bells.
I almost feel the way I did as a child, dancing.

Govinda says, as though he can read my mind,
"That's what the best dancers do.
They focus on dance.

They forget their feet, their bodies,
their dancer selves.
They let dance tug their souls upward.
And as they rise,
they lift their audiences closer to heaven, too."

ABSOLUTE

Joyful music plays in my head all the next day. But
when I come home from school,
an ambulance is screeching
away from our building.
"Paati collapsed," I hear Ma say.
"Pa's in the ambulance with her."

The music stops.

Mrs. Subramaniam runs out of her apartment.
I hear her shocked voice
asking what happened, which hospital.
Calling a taxi to rush us there.

My tongue is frozen.
Chandra told me once about absolute zero,
a temperature cold enough to bring
the universe to a standstill.
My heart feels like it's at absolute zero.

Pa meets me and Ma in the hospital waiting room,
his cheeks shrunk with worry.
Heart attack, he says, but she survived.
Thank God. Ma sobs.
Pa and Ma lean against one another.
Shivering, I sink into a chair.

NIGHT

My room feels deathly silent
without Paati's breath lulling me to sleep.

I run my fingertips over the feet
of my bronze statue of Shiva dancing
on the table between our beds.
"Please. Let Paati come back home."
Moonlight drips into the dark room.
I slip out of bed, crawl on the floor,
yank open the metal trunk beneath Paati's bed,
in which she stores her things,
and drink in the soothing basil-aloe scent of her soap.
Paati's saris glow,
a shell-bright patch of white.
I take a sari out of the trunk.
Lay it on my pillow.
Bury my face in it.
Let it soak up my tears.
Bathed in her fragrance and her softness,
I drift toward sleep.

GHOST WHITE

Lying in her hospital bed, in her white sari,
Paati looks like a ghost.
I rub her fingers. "Are you in pain? How are you feeling?"
"Well enough to get out of here soon.
Tell me about you," Paati says.
I half sob, half laugh with relief. "I'm okay."
"Tell me more or I'll throw you out myself," she says.
"Paati, I'm waiting for you to come back. I miss you so much
I've been praying to my Shiva at night."
Paati circles my wrist with her fingers. Her touch is frail
but her eyes brighten and she says, "Good."
I stroke the folds of skin on her cheeks, her forehead,
the silvery strands of her hair spread out on the pillow,
thin as strips of moonlight on a cloud.
A nurse pokes in, saying
an old student of Paati's wants to see her,
can she let the woman in?
"So many years since I taught.
Yet students keep remembering and returning with love.
Maybe you should try teaching dance someday.

Maybe if I've accumulated enough good Karma,
I'll be one of your students in my next life." She chuckles.
I don't. I don't want to think about Paati's future lives.
I'm just glad she's still here, near me,
in this one.

THE DANCE
of
ATOMS

Chandra comes over to ask about Paati.
I ask her to go to the temple with me
so we can pray for Paati's health.
We walk past the empty lot
where Paati and I met the beggar
who wished me better Karma in my next life.
Lightning and thunder rip the sky.
Within moments, the road turns into a brown river.
Plastic bags, banana peels, coconut husks
float on the dirty water like disoriented boats.

Chandra and I shelter
under the eaves of a nearby fruit vendor's hut.
Craning my neck,
I see the beggar
crouched beneath his tarpaulin, shivering.

I have so much, even though I lost a leg.
I have Chandra walking beside me,

Govinda helping me relearn what I love,
Ma and Pa both supporting me,
Paati still alive and soon to return home.
But the question I asked Paati returns to me.
Why did God leave that beggar with nothing?
"Chandra, do you believe in God? In Karma?
If He's the soul of compassion, why does He let people suffer?"
Chandra shrugs.
"Physics says every action has an equal and opposite reaction.
Karma is kind of the same, isn't it?
Good actions result in rewards, sooner or later.
If you cause suffering, instead, something bad will return to you.
As for God, the fact that atoms are inside everything
tells me God is within us all.
I see His cosmic dance of creation as
the spinning of electrons within every atom.
Science is God enough for me."
But not
for me.

I think of the last time I was at this temple with Paati,
her silver head bent in prayer, so empowered by her faith.
The image of her, so sure, so firm in her belief,
gives me comfort.
And though I'm not sure what God means to me
or if He hears me,
I pray as hard as I can
for Paati's safe return home.

SEEING
SHIVA

Home from the hospital,
Paati can no longer pray sitting cross-legged
on the floor in front of our household altar.
I offer to bring the other deities to our bedside table
where my Shiva dances.
Paati shakes her head.
So instead, I fetch the bottle of oil.
As I massage her,
Paati says, "Objects of prayer used to help me focus my mind.
I don't need them anymore.
Shiva dances everywhere.
In everyone. In everything."

DANCE
YOGA

In class with Govinda,
I fall almost at once.
He pulls me to my feet,
his eyebrows furrowed with worry. "Something's wrong."

"My grandma had a heart attack.
She's home now, but I'm so scared—" My voice breaks.
He strokes my back. "I'm glad she's better now."
His voice is a soothing balm.

I add, "Akka says I'm clearly showing my pain,
but not the peace Gautami found after accepting her loss.
I don't feel peaceful, Govinda.
I can't show what I don't know."

Govinda stands erect.
Starts
moving
slower than I thought possible.
Watching his body flow

from one pose to the next,

moving in concert with the rise and fall of his chest,

is as calming

as watching clouds drift across a blue sky.

"Dance is a form of yoga. *Natya* yoga," he says.

"Marry your movement with your breath.

Rest your palms on mine." He extends his hands toward me,

his palms beneath mine,

offering gentle support.

I discover it isn't easy to dance so slowly.

If anything, it's harder than going fast.

When I go slow, every asymmetry is magnified.

"Veda? Don't worry about how you look.

About anything."

Breath for deep breath, I match Govinda.

Inhale. Exhale. Inhale.

We breathe as one.

Our paired breath is the only sound in the room.

"Some of us meditate through movement," Govinda says.

"Meditation isn't about pushing your body,

it's about respecting it,

the way you'd respect

every other space within which God dwells."

My breath doesn't race
like it used to when I danced fast and furious.
There's no rush of blood to my head.
No gush of excitement in my chest.
Dancing slowly makes a new feeling
of joy enter my body.
A joy that seems longer lasting
than the bubbles of delight that rose within me
when I danced in the past.

As I relax, I sense how tightly I'd reeled in my chest,
holding myself as tensely as a warrior queen,
charging into battle,
weighted down by armor.

I feel
Govinda peeling
my armor away.

INVITED

After dance rehearsal, Radhika invites me
to her birthday party.
"I live next door to Govinda.
He'll be there," she says.
A pang of jealousy pricks me like a needle
but she adds, as if to reassure me, "He's like my brother.
We've been neighbors since we were three."
I feel relieved,
until she says, "I've never seen him so crazy
about any other girl."
He was crazy about other girls? Who? I can't help feeling
another jab of envy.

"Party?" Pa rolls the word in his mouth
when I ask permission to go. "Party? Girls only?"
"Only a few boys. From the dance class. Please?"
I don't remember begging for anything else.
Ma tells Pa, "It's during the *day*.
At a *girl's* home. Her *parents* will be there.
And that nice boy, Govinda, whom we met.

Of course she should go."

Forced to agree with Ma, Pa says yes.

I thank him.

And fling my arms around Ma.

TOAD
in a
LOTUS LAKE

In the over-cooled air of Radhika's parents' mansion,
after my hot, dusty bus ride,
I shiver.
My loose kurti shirt and long salwar trousers
look frumpy
compared to the tight tops and short skirts
every other girl seems to be wearing.
And I feel flat-footed as they tower over me
in high heels that *clip-clop* across the marble floor.
I want to run out the carved front door
at which I left my slippers the way I would
at any normal Indian home,
instead of keeping them on like the others have
as though we're in some hotel.

My naked toes curl and dig into my foot.
I feel uglier and more out of place
than a warty toad stuck in a lake full of lotuses.

DIFFERENT
DANCES

"Veda! I was waiting for you."
Govinda offers me the warmth of his hand and I take it.
He leads me up a sweep of stairs
into a sun-soaked hall where music's playing
and all the furniture's pushed against walls.
Radhika spots me and gives me a hug.
"Thanks so much for coming."
She looks lovely
in a curve-hugging dress and high-heeled sandals,
her dimpled cheeks accented with rouge.
Even her toes look perfect—
painted with a soft pink nail polish.

"Dance?" Govinda asks me.
"Don't know how," I say.
Radhika giggles. "You
don't know how
to dance?"
"Not to this music, I don't."

"Good thing your teacher is here." Radhika gives me
a playful shove. "Lesson time, Veda."

Govinda pulls me to the middle of the room.
"Put your arms on my shoulders.
Now move. With me."
I sense where he wants me to go
through the tensing and easing of his muscles.
It feels like learning a new language.

I remember daydreaming of dancing this way with Jim.
My stomach clenches with guilt.
But only for a moment.
Jim feels long ago and far away.
I feel the way I did when my cracked ribs finally healed:
delighted to discover there's no longer any pain in my chest.
"Something wrong?" Govinda says. "Did I step on your foot?"
"If you did,
it was the foot that doesn't hurt," I say.
He smiles.
Dazzling as polished topaz,
the tiny gold flecks in Govinda's eyes
catch and toss
sunlight.

SACRED
WATER

Paati's tortured breathing wakes me.
A cool predawn breeze shivers in through our window
but sweat lathers Paati's forehead.
She mumbles something,
her words slurred, her eyes unfocused.
"Pa! Ma! Come quickly!"
I grab my crutches, then, realizing I need to use my hands,
I get my leg on instead
and hurry to fetch the small sealed pot
filled with water from the sacred Ganga river.
A copper pot that's sat in a corner of our household altar
for as long as I can remember.
Waiting for a time of death.
I know Paati will want a drink of this water
from the holiest of rivers.
She believes it will help wash away her sins.
Though I don't believe she sinned in this life,
I break open the seal and
dash back to our bedroom,
Ganga water sloshing.

Paati's drawn cheeks
crease into a faint smile.
For a moment her eyes clear.
Her lips part.
I splash some water into her mouth.
She swallows.
My arms tremble.
I pour an unsteady stream on her tongue.
She lifts a hand
as if to touch my cheek
but her hand falls back
on her chest.
Her lips close.
The last of the water
spills on her chin and dribbles
down her neck.

Ma leans forward.
Shuts Paati's eyelids.
Slides her arms around Pa.
Pa covers his face with his hands.

STRANGE COMFORT

My body feels heavy
but I go to Pa
and stroke his shaking shoulders.

When the heart-shaped leaves
of the pipul tree outside our window
start sifting through the rays of the rising sun,
Ma leaves the room.
I hear her on the phone, telling people Paati's gone.

I stay with Pa.
Hug him tight.
Feel his tears wet my curls as he cries into my hair.
"Paati would have wanted to die this way," I tell him. "Quietly.
At home. In her bed. The three of us close by."
He nods, still hunched over.

Finally,
he says, "I didn't think of the Ganga water.
I'm glad you remembered."

Tears well up within me
but they can't find their way out.

Day breaks in
through the window.
A bucket of gold melting from the sky.

Visitors gather on the sitting room floor in a circle:
the Subramaniams and our other neighbors;
three old students of Paati's;
Pa's and Ma's colleagues;
members of Pa's extended family.

Chandra arrives with her grandma, parents, and sisters.
I lean my head against Chandra's shoulder.
Still, I'm unable to weep.

People speak about Paati's kindness,
her helpfulness, her wonderful cooking,
how brave she was, how unusual a widow for her time,
how her firm faith inspired them.
One of Paati's old students says,
"She taught us not only in class,
but also by setting us an example
of how to act in our lives."

Mrs. Subramaniam says,
"Your paati treated everyone so lovingly

I'm sure her soul doesn't need to be reborn in the world.
She'll now be united with God."

Listening to stranger after stranger
speak of Paati with love and admiration,
I begin to understand how Gautami
took comfort in the tales of strangers
after she lost her son.

The strangers' presence feels warm as a blanket.
But not warm enough
to thaw the sea of unshed tears
frozen inside me.

SWOLLEN

After
Pa leaves with Paati's body for the cremation ground,
others leave but Chandra stays.
She helps
me and Ma clean the house.

Ma is afraid I'll slip and hurt myself
but I mop the floor of what is now
just—my—bedroom.
Crawling on hands and knees
I dip a sponge in soapy water,
scrub the tiles, wring it dry.

Chandra's cheeks glisten.
Wet as the mopped floor.

I'm a soaked sponge.
Swollen with tears.

A TIME
to
DANCE

I mail Govinda and akka a note
to say I won't be at our dance school
until Paati's twelve-day mourning period has ended.

A condolence card arrives
signed by akka, Radhika, and Govinda.

Govinda alone also sends a letter.
Dear Veda,
The verse below is from the Bible, not a Hindu text, but
it helped me when my favorite aunt died.

> *To every thing there is a season,*
>> *and a time to every purpose under Heaven:*
> *A time to be born, and a time to die;*
>> *a time to plant, and a time to reap;*
> *A time to kill, and a time to heal;*
>> *a time to break down, and a time to build up;*
> *A time to weep, and a time to laugh;*
>> *a time to mourn, and a time to dance . . .*

Whenever you feel it's time to dance again,
I'll be here, waiting.
Love,
Govinda.

I sleep with Govinda's letter
under my pillow.

HOLDING ON

For twelve days,
priests light a ceremonial fire in the center of our hall.
For twelve days,
priests guide Pa as he performs Paati's final rites.
They pray to Shiva, creator of worlds, destroyer of evil.
He is bliss, they say.
From joy were we made,
by joy do we live,
and unto joy
do we return.

Pa mouths the prayers.
I can't tell if he takes any comfort in them.
The words fall with dull thuds on my ears.

On the thirteenth day, Pa's family from far away joins us.
We feast together and then they leave and the priests leave.
Pa says, "It's time we collected all of Paati's things
to give to the poor."
But when he comes to my room to take Paati's trunk away,
I throw myself over it,

shouting, "No!"

Tears burst out of me.

"It's the custom," Pa says, gently. "Giving her things

away to charity

is a tradition she'd want us to follow.

It doesn't mean we'll forget her."

An endless stream of tears

pours down my face.

Ma rubs my back.

Pa returns the trunk to its place under Paati's bed.

But I can't

stop

sobbing.

VISITATION

A ghost visits me that night.
Not Paati. I'd have welcomed her.
Instead, the lost length of leg beneath my knee
prickles.
An invisible reincarnation
taunting me.

Worse than any ghost story Paati told,
this haunting phantom flesh.

My moans bring Ma and Pa rushing to my bed.
They can't exorcise my pain.
Not even Paati could.
But I long to feel
her touch.

FIGHTING
PHANTOMS

Our doorbell rings. I hear Govinda's voice.
Before I can pull my leg on,
he's standing outside my bedroom door,
saying, "I wanted to make sure you were okay."

I feel caught unawares, holding my unnatural limb in my hands,
like a murderer dismembering a corpse.

Pain from my phantom limb
pierces me.
As if a million fire ants are stinging my nonexistent skin.

Govinda runs to my side.
"Veda? What's wrong? Tell me."

"My
right foot
hurts."
Gasps punctuate my words.
I grimace with pain from the ghost neither of us can see.

"Ever had your leg go to sleep?
Go numb for a while and later tingle back to life?
Like that. Only my leg's amputated.
So it hurts worse."

Govinda kneels.
"Where's the pain?" He molds my hand onto his. "Show me."
I guide his fingers over my ghostly foot.
I watch him
pressing my invisible ankle,
rubbing my invisible instep,
kneading my invisible toes
as though he can sense it as clearly as I can.

My ghost pain fades.
Bizarre.
"Thanks." I shudder,
feeling like a monster.
A half leg of my own,
an artificial leg that can never feel,
an imaginary leg taunting my brain,
and one normal leg.
"I'm a four-legged beast.
Not a dancer."

"The divine dancer has four arms,"
Govinda says.
He chants,

"Yatho hasta thatho drishti; Yatho drishti thatho manah;
Yatho manah thatho bhaavah; Yatho bhaavah thatho rasa."
The hand leads the eyes; the eyes lead the mind;
the mind leads emotional expression;
emotion leads to experience.
No mention of feet
ghostly or real.

Govinda says, "People forget what they see onstage.
They remember only how deeply you touched their feelings.
Akka can dance even if she's seated the entire time.
The best dancers
can move an audience
without once moving their own feet."

Govinda flattens my palms, fingers together,
straight except for the thumb;
shaping my hand into *Pataaka hasta*—my first hand word—
a symbol that can show many things.
He places my palms
together like the two leaves of a closed door.
Turns them gently apart to show the door opening.

Then he links one of his hands with one of mine,
interlocking our thumbs,
forging them into the wings of the divine eagle, Garuda.
Our feet are still. But we're dancing.

Our fingers flutter.
Our wings flap.
Our divine eagle flies.
Higher and higher.
Glides.
Soars.

THE COLOR
of
MUSIC

⁕⁓⁓⁊   ⁊⁓⁓⁕

Outside the window of akka's study,
gray clouds smear the sky like ash.
I tell Govinda, "I wish we didn't cremate our dead.
So I could at least have a grave to visit.
But my pa scattered Paati's ashes
in the Adayar river, as she wanted."

Govinda doesn't give me the usual reply—
that to hold on to someone's mortal remains
is to dishonor their eternal soul.
Instead he says, "Would you like to go
to where her ashes are, Veda?
The river-mouth is near here."

Govinda walks me
to the Theosophical society—a green oasis in the city—
along the banks of the Adayar river.
Scattered inside the grounds,

between acres of trees,
are a few old Victorian villas
and several places of worship: a church, a mosque, a synagogue,
a Hindu temple.

Govinda and I stand together on the sandy shore
of the Adayar estuary,
where the river that bore Paati's ashes rushes toward the sea.
I think of a prayer Paati used to say,
that each soul has a different path to reach God
just as each river takes a different course to the one great ocean.

"Maybe Paati's soul is with God and I can't sense her presence
because I haven't figured out what God is," I tell Govinda.

A light drizzle wets the earth. Raindrops
split sunlight into bands of separate color.
White light—one color containing myriad others—
I understand.
Water—one substance with many forms—I can feel.
God—one yet infinite in form—I can't understand.

"When I dance," Govinda says,
"or when I'm in a beautiful place,
I feel I'm in the presence of something
large and good.
It doesn't give me answers. But I don't need them.

For me that feeling
of wonder, of awe, of mystery,
of being in touch with something larger,
is as close as God comes."

Wonder. Mystery. Awe.
In touch with something large and good.
The way I felt as a child in the temple of the dancing Shiva,
exploring every crevice of His sculpted feet with my fingertips.
I had no questions then. Only a yearning to learn dance.
I have questions now. But perhaps I don't need answers.
Like Gautami, who, in the end, didn't need an explanation
for her son's death, because she found
experiencing Buddha's compassion was enough.
Perhaps even God doesn't know
why some suffer more, some less.

Paati seemed sure what God meant to her.
Maybe, like Govinda, I don't need to be sure.
Maybe all I need is to feel what I felt as a child. Through dance.
By dancing a different way,
dancing so it strengthens not just my body,
but also helps me find, then soothe, and strengthen, my soul.

CLOSE

Govinda and I arrive at a pond filled with dark pink lotuses.
"This is my temple," Govinda says.
He sits next to me on the grassy bank.
There's a space between us, a sliver of air.
He held my waist the day of the party.
Now, with no one else nearby,
with no excuse to touch me, he's careful and correct.
I love that he's such a gentleman.
I hate that he's such a gentleman.

While we sit together, sharing silence,
my impatience slowly falls away.
Music enters my mind,
notes as sweet as I always heard as a child.
A frog hops onto the grass, *tha thing gina thom.*
In the distance, a woodpecker raps at a tree trunk,
tha thai tha, dhit thai tha.

Govinda whispers, *"Tha thai tha, dhit thai tha."*
He's saying aloud
the same rhythm I hear in my head.

"Veda, can you hear it?
Music to dance to. All around us."

"I hear it."
I feel closer to him
than if we were in one another's arms.

A PART

The evening of our performance
as a minor player in the large sweep of a dance production
the nervousness I feel is not for myself
but for Govinda, who is in the lead,
and for Radhika and all the others
who stay longer onstage than I do.

Akka lights a lamp backstage and we bow to it.

When it's my turn,
my right foot leads my left
onto the stage
into the pain
I felt when my body and part of my life
were torn away.

My back hunched, I play the woman
overcome by age and illness.
In the scrape of the cane I hold,
I hear the echo of my crutches.

In my second role, as Gautami, I hold
not the body of my lost child,
but my severed limb.

When Gautami is comforted by strangers,
I hear the words strangers said to me after Paati's death,
and feel a sense of peace.

Dhanam akka nods and gives me quick pat on the shoulder.
Radhika hugs me and says I was "amazing."
Govinda's little sister, Leela, joins me in the wings.
Together, we watch the rest of the play.

At the end of the evening,
Govinda leads me onstage with him,
ahead of the rest of the cast
despite my minor role.
Standing together in a group, we press our palms together
and bow our heads to salute the audience.
When our shared applause comes,
it feels like being part of a winning cricket team,
only far, far better.
Because I'm part of a dance team,
together with people who share my love of dance.

TO STAND

I find Govinda slumped in a chair when I enter akka's study
for our first class together after our performance.
I can't imagine why he looks so defeated.
"Govinda? You were wonderful onstage."

He doesn't seem to hear me.
"My parents want me to cut back on dance
now that the production is over.
To work with a tutor.
Prepare for college entrance tests.
Become an engineer.
I don't know how I can argue anymore—"
He breaks off and stares at the carpet.

It was hard enough for me just fighting my ma,
having Pa and Paati supporting me.
Govinda has no one in his family backing him up.
I put my hands on his shoulders.

"On top of it all," Govinda says,
"there's a new beginner class I'm supposed to teach.

I don't want to give up my own dance lessons with akka—
but there's not enough time to do everything."

"What if I teach your beginner class
so you don't have to give up your own—" I stop short,
shocked by my own words.
Me? A teacher? What am I thinking?

Govinda straightens up as if I lifted a load
off his back.
"That's a great idea. You'd be good for the kids.
You'll love teaching. And I could use the extra time to study."
Every trace of dullness leaves him.
He looks so relieved
that I can't take back my offer.
"Thanks, Veda.
Thanks so much. Let's talk to akka."

Hoping akka will refuse to let me teach,
I follow Govinda out of the study.

Unfortunately, akka seems pleased I volunteered
to help him out.
"One learns best through teaching," she says.
"I'm glad you'd like to teach dance, Veda."

TEACHING
to
LEARN

A roomful of eager eyes turns toward me.

My voice trembles. "Namaskaram.

My name is Veda." I think of the grace with which

Govinda imbued that word and gesture the first time we met.

The only little boy in class is first to introduce himself.

"My name is Roshan," he says, his round face beaming.

He's followed by six small, excited girls.

Only one girl hangs back,

a faded scarf covering her mouth and chin

despite the heat.

"What's your name?" I approach her,

hoping to make her feel welcome.

Her ragged clothes suggest she's one of the poorer students.

"Uma," she answers, a cautious look in her large eyes,

her scarf muffling her voice.

Is she hiding her face

because she's painfully shy?

I teach the children the starting prayer,
show them how to do the first exercise.

Sitting cross-legged on the floor,
I wipe my sweaty palm dry on my skirt.
I'm not scared to tap out basic rhythms. I know how.
I'm not even worried about how I'll look dancing
the basic exercises in front of the children;
I can manage all of them, if imperfectly.
What frightens me is living up to the example Govinda set.
Govinda, so generous, caring, concerned.

Paati's voice whispers in my mind. "I was a teacher.
Your pa is a teacher. It's in your blood."

Clutching the stick with both hands,
I tap out the first rhythm in first speed.
Thaiya thai, thaiya thai.
Repeating the rhythm, my voice and my hands grow steady.

After class, I look for Uma,
who hid half her face behind her scarf
the entire time she danced.
She's disappeared.

DRIVE

Govinda's usually in akka's study waiting for me
well ahead of our class time.
But I rush in
eager to tell him
how my classes with the children are going,
only to find the room empty.

I look out the window.
See a figure running up the drive.
But it's not Govinda.
Govinda's never late.
Maybe he's caught in traffic.
Or—what if—
A sickening fear slithers in the pit of my stomach.
I pace the room for what feels like forever
but the clock tells me is only ten minutes.

Akka enters the study.
"Govinda's on the phone for you."

"Govinda, I was so worried!
Thank goodness you're all right.
What happened? Where are you?"

"Veda, I'm really, really sorry.
I can't come today.
My parents arranged for a tutor to coach me at home.
He went on and on. We lost track of time.
I should have called sooner."

Pretending I'm patient,
trying to be there for him like he always was for me,
I hold back the anger
that's swirling up inside me like a dancer's skirts.
"It's okay," I say. "I understand."

SEEING I

I catch Uma
as she tries to run out the door after class.
"Why do you always
hide your face?" I ask. "You should take off the scarf
and free up your neck."

Her eyes fill with tears. "Please,
don't be angry.
I love dance."

"Then show us your face so we can see how much you love it.
Dancers don't hang their heads."

Uma starts to turn her head away,
but I cup her chin
and her scarf slips a few inches lower.
Enough to unveil her cleft lip.
"I want to dance," she says,
"but I'm not pretty enough to show my face.
Please let me keep my scarf."
Tears shine like diamonds caught in her thick, long lashes.

"Uma, you're safe here. I'd never let anyone tease you.
I promise you'll feel graceful and beautiful
if you dance freely."

But Uma ties her scarf
tight around her mouth.

Next class, Uma still hangs her head
and dances, face half-hidden,
looking as unsure of herself
as she did on the first day.

PRESENT

I'm walking toward akka's study
for class with Govinda
when akka meets me and hands me an envelope.
"Something small, a little early—
for your upcoming birthday."

Stammering thanks, I drop the envelope, shocked.
I didn't know she knew my birthday.
She flicks her hand as though swatting away a mosquito.
"Consider it an assignment, Veda.
There's a dance recital I want you to attend
ahead of your birthday.
Whirling Sufi dervishes will perform.
And non-classical dancers of other faiths and traditions.
Watching them will teach you something, I hope."

I slit the envelope to find three tickets.
Akka explains, "I thought Govinda might join you.
And I presume if you went out with a boy in the evening,
your parents would prefer if someone else came along."

I can't wait to invite Govinda.
But I'm forced to.

Apologizing, Govinda rushes into the study.
Late.
Half an hour late.

I shove the tickets akka gave me
away in my bag.

STRONG
QUIET

Roshan, the only boy in class, surprises me
by entering stealthily,
his shoulders slumped,
his neck drooping almost as low as Uma's always does.

I crouch beside him and ask what's wrong.
He tells me, "My big brother said
strong boys do sports. Real boys don't dance."

"He's wrong, Roshan. Strong boys are brave enough
to fight for what they want.
Strong boys care about Karma and what's right,
not following the crowd.
You tell that to anyone who says
you're weak because you like dance. Okay?"

My words seem to reach Roshan.
He rapidly bounces
back to his normal, cheerful self.

PLACES
of
PRAYER

I open Paati's prayer books,
dust off her brass bell,
light a stick of incense,
and sit cross-legged
on the ground in front of our household altar
although it's hard to do with my prosthesis.

I pray I'll find a way
to help Uma
find happiness and confidence through dance.
And I pray I'll find my way
through my tangled mess of feelings for Govinda.

Not a flicker of light penetrates through my confusion.
But if nothing else,
if Paati's soul hasn't been reincarnated in another body,
if she's out there somewhere watching me,
she'd be happy seeing me fill our house with prayer.

Wherever she is now,
maybe my voice can reach her.

Pa joins me on the floor in front of the altar.
He thanks me
for keeping Paati's traditions alive in our home.
He says he's glad she planted her faith inside me.

SKIRT

Ironing the hem of my school skirt,
I tell Chandra about the three tickets
akka gave me for the concert.
"You'll come, won't you?"

"So I can hold one of your hands while Govinda holds the other?"
Suppressed laughter leaps in Chandra's eyes.

The iron hisses. "I'm not sure he likes me that way, Chandra.
He's always busy. Studying.
Maybe I mistook Govinda's feelings for me
like I misread Jim's.
Imagining there's something between us
though all Govinda sees in me is a friend."

"Studying for college entrance tests is tough, Veda.
What d'you think I'm doing when you're off dancing?
Working as hard as I can to make good grades."

"You still make time for me.
Govinda cancels classes. Or comes late."

"He's probably just having trouble
fitting things into his new schedule.
I've given up cricket so I can study every spare minute.
Govinda could have given up your classes together,
but he's trying to manage everything, isn't he?
Studying for college, teaching you,
and keeping up with his own dance lessons."

The skirt has a stubborn crease.
I press it out with my steaming iron.
Chandra's right.
Govinda has done—is still trying to do—a lot for me.

Chandra folds my shirt, puts it away.
"Are you having fun teaching?" she asks.
I tell her about Uma.
"I'm sure her parents are too poor to pay for an operation.
She loves dance, but doesn't do it right
because she's trying so hard to hide her mouth.
I wish I could get her to feel
safe enough in class to not worry.
But I don't know how to help her. I'm a useless teacher."

Chandra marches to my dresser. Rummages through.
Yanks out the short blue batik skirt I bought
last time we went shopping together.
When I had two real legs.

She fingers the price tag. "Brand-new.
You've never worn this skirt?"

My iron splutters. I turn it off.
"What does that skirt have to do with anything?"

"You're always covering up your leg
but you want to teach Uma she's not ugly?"
Chandra throws the skirt at me.

The silky fabric is rumpled
from being squashed in the back of a drawer.
I smooth out the wrinkles,
spread the skirt flat on my ironing table.
Turn my iron back on.

STRENGTH

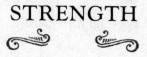

Govinda arrives
only a little late.
Apologizing as usual.

"I hate studying," he adds, quietly.
"I miss being with you like we used to.
Wish I could study less and dance more."
He misses being with me!

"Govinda, akka gave me tickets. To a dance recital.
Can you come?"

Without even checking his calendar, he shakes his head.
"I'm so sorry, Veda. I wish I could.
My parents wouldn't understand
if I took an entire evening off for a dance concert.
Not right now."

After those magical moments we shared by the lotus pond,
both hearing the same music in our minds;

after dancing so close together at Radhika's party
—was I wrong to feel our friendship
was deepening into more?

"Veda, I'm so behind on mathematics.
I have so much to catch up on.
I love dance. But it isn't my life."
Govinda sounds like he's reading a speech
written by someone else,
trying to convince himself it's true,
and failing.

"What is your life, Govinda?
Whatever your parents tell you it should be?"

"Veda, please. Try to understand," he pleads,
"I like you. A lot. But I'm not like you."

Didn't I want Govinda to say he liked me?
Shouldn't I be happy?
But the moment feels all wrong.
I want him to repeat it,
say it strongly.
Wanting him to reassure me
that he likes me enough
he'll never give up our time together,
I say, "I can work on my own, Govinda.
So you'll have more time to study."

But my words
don't work the way I want.

Govinda nods. Says softly, "It's probably good
for you to work on your own for a while.
We'll still find ways to meet.
I promise."

I shrug
as though
I don't care
if we see each other again.
Because I feel
like a heap of discarded clothing.

RED DOT

That night, I crawl to Paati's trunk
and I take one of her saris back to bed with me.
Paati was soft—soft as her sari.
Yet also strong.
Govinda's softness I love,
but his caving in to his parents I don't even like.
His need to please them seems stronger
than his need—for dance and me—both.
Unable to sleep, I twist and untwist the fabric.

My phantom comes alive.
Beneath my right knee,
nails scratch at invisible skin.
I bite down. Sweat beads on my lips.
I bolt upright and grip my residual limb.
This is all I have.
My pain is an illusion.
I will not give in.

A beam of moonlight gleams through the bronze circle of flame
in which my Shiva dances.

Shiva, I pray,
open my third eye.
Help me sense the truth
and drive away this unreal pain.
Open my third eye.
Show me your light.
And let me see
Govinda's feelings for me
and mine for him
clearly.

I press on the spot between my brows.
Desperate.
My forehead wet with sweat.
Concentrate.
Reality is the pressure between my eyebrows.

Next morning, I see a red dot
bored into the skin at the center of my forehead
by my fingernail.

HAUNTED

Chandra knows right away something's wrong
when we meet for lunch at school.
"What's the matter, Veda? Someone say something?
Need me to punch the terrible twins?"

"Govinda said he liked me
but I messed it all up, Chandra.
Acted like I didn't care
if we never met again."

"So call him and apologize.
It's as easy as that," Chandra says.

"But it—scares me
how Govinda gives in to his parents.
What if Govinda and I get together
and his parents don't like me?
Will
he give me up, too,
like that rich boy who dumped your sister?"

"Not every rich boy is an invertebrate like my sister's ex.
And look at your ma. She married your pa
though her family said no."

"My ma admitted she still misses her family.
It takes a lot of strength to do what she did."
My voice shakes. "Chandra, I don't know what to do.
I miss him. I'm so confused."

"You'll work it out," Chandra says.
I'm not sure if she means
Govinda and I will work things out together
or if she means
I'll work him out of my system.

OFFERING
THANKS

I'm practicing on my own at home
trying not to think how much I miss Govinda,
when our doorbell rings.

I'm surprised to find our neighbors
Mrs. Subramaniam and her daughter
standing on the landing.
"We have something for you," Shobana says.

"For me?"
All these years the Subramaniams lived below us,
I never once thought of getting anything
for them.

"After your accident, we prayed for your recovery,"
Mrs. Subramaniam says.
"We saw you onstage again,
at the performance about Buddha's life.
So we went to the temple and offered thanks."

Shobana gives me a package of blessed food
and a packet of vermillion powder.
"Here is some *prasadam* from the temple.
And some *kumkumam*."

"Thank you."
How do I apologize
for being so involved with my own dance
that I never found time to talk with them?

Shobana waves her hand at me
as though waving away my thanks.
She and her mother disappear down the stairs.

Guilt makes
the packets they gave me
feel heavier than rocks.

FINDING
MY WAY

Every time the phone rings, I hope it's Govinda.
It never is.
Every time I enter dance school,
my eyes search for some sign of him.
He's nowhere to be seen.

So I find Radhika,
and ask her to come to the concert with me and Chandra.
Radhika tucks an arm through mine and she
tugs me toward the empty stage under the banyan tree.

"Veda? I've known Govinda all my life.
He's crazy about you."

"He doesn't act like he cares, Radhika.
I asked him out to the concert
and he turned me down.
He hasn't called since.
Has he given up dance altogether? Is he avoiding me?"

I cross my arms over my chest
like that will help me
hold myself together.

Radhika gives me a quick hug.
"Veda, I think it was good for Govinda that you two fought.
He's sorting out his life right now.
I can't tell you a whole lot—but, yes,
he's in touch with akka still.
He's not given up dance altogether.
And trust me—he really likes you.
So if you like him, too, you'll surely get back together.
Wait and see."

A GIFT

The smell of semolina and cardamom and melting butter
surprises me when I return home.
Ma is back early, making hot sojji
like Paati used to.
"Thanks, Ma."
My voice falters.
The spicy-sweet scent
makes me miss Paati.

"Not as good as your grandmother's."
Ma piles some on a plate.
I taste a spoonful.
"Different.
But also very good."

Ma gazes at the steam
rising from the cooling mass of semolina.
"I wish your pa and I had been able to work less.
Spend more time with Paati and you.
Your paati was a pillar at the center of our household.
I never saw her death coming.

I let her do too much.
I never saw her age."

"She wouldn't acknowledge her age either," I say.
"She never enjoyed people fussing over her.
She would have hated it if you'd tried to make her rest.
She wouldn't have wanted it any other way."

Ma's eyes are tearful
but she smiles as if I've given her a gift.

SHARING

Ma's made so much sojji there's a huge mound left.
I decide to take some to our neighbors downstairs.
Ringing their doorbell
—after ignoring them all my life—
feels strange.
But Mrs. Subramaniam
welcomes me in
with nothing but friendliness in her tone.
Mr. Subramaniam says, "So nice you're here, Veda."
And Shobana's eyes light up.

In one corner of the room, inside a glass-fronted cupboard,
I see a beautiful old veena, its seven strings
glinting as though someone just oiled them.
"Do you play the veena?" I ask Shobana.

"Yes, want to listen?" Shobana unrolls a straw mat,
places her veena on the ground,
and sits cross-legged in front of it, caressing the strings.
She loves music as I love dance.

"Shobana, perhaps you can practice what you plan to play
for the boy's family this weekend," her mother suggests.
She tells me a nice boy
is coming with his family to "see" Shobana
to decide whether she's a good match,
in as old-fashioned a way as in Paati's day.
Even Chandra's family, though traditional enough
to set up a meeting for her sister with a boy they approve of,
will at least give the couple
the freedom to meet alone for some time
and choose whether to marry.

I glance at Shobana's face.
I don't know her enough to tell if she's upset.
From her veena's strings, she plucks
the pensive notes of a sad but hopeful key:
Raagam Hamsaanandi.
Listening to the mood of her music shivering in the room,
I pray that Shobana's husband will be a good, kind man.
And that he'll share her love of music.

SILENCE
SOUNDS

Roshan prances from the classroom, the last child to leave.
As I follow him out, I hear
Govinda say,
"How are you, Veda? How is everything?"
He looks more beautiful
and sounds more caring than ever.
I feel like I've stepped into a strong current of water,
pulling me toward him.

I wonder if Govinda was teased about dance, too.
He probably had to learn to stand up to other boys,
just as Roshan must.
Govinda must have a strength
I never recognized.

I want to voice my thoughts but they stay trapped in my mind.
Chained feet that can't escape.

We fall into that unhappy place
where words are snatched away
and silence feels loud.

"See you later?"
Govinda leaves me
wishing I'd said, "Let's meet.
Soon."

FROM DANCER
to
DANCE

Radhika and Chandra come with me
to the evening of "transcendental dance"
for which Dhanam akka's given us tickets
in the very front row.

On an open-air stage,
I see a dancer—a very old woman.
She wears long, loose, saffron-colored robes. No jewelry.
White locks wave wildly all about her face.
Her eyes look
at us
at me
at something beyond.
I see nothing but the darkness of the evening.
She sings, "What Your name is, I do not know or care.
Because I feel You everywhere I dance."
Her notes rise into the air.
She follows her voice with her body,
turning slowly, her arms outstretched like beams of light

reaching upward from the earth.
Her palms carve a staircase into the sky.
I watch her skirts swirling around her ankles,
her hair flying around her face,
whirling faster than the rest of her.
She is the edge of a spinning circle.
She is the stillness at its center.
She is light as a petal rising in a spiraling breeze.
She is a petal dissolving into flower-dust.
Disappearing.

On the stage,
there is no dancer.
There is
only dance.

MY WAY TO PRAY

At home, bowing to my dancing Shiva,
I say silently
the words of the prayer Govinda taught me.
My hands are lips.
My body is voice.

As I shape the words
"the entire universe is His body"
an invisible hand flicks on the switch I've been fumbling with.

In my mind's eye, I see my students.
See the strength, the weakness, the curve of each back,
the slope of each shoulder.
Elbows with a natural bend.
Upper bodies that jut out too far forward
as though they're trying to race ahead of the feet.
No body perfect.
No two children the same size or shape.
But every dancing child a manifestation
of Shiva in human form.

LETTING GO

The morning of my birthday,
I ask Pa to come to the temple with me,
where I've gone with Paati every birthday morning
before this one.

In the vacant lot where the beggar lived,
I see a scrawny boy dressed in a filthy T-shirt.
He tears a thin roti in half,
holds the bread out
to feed a stray dog.

"Pa," I say, "I don't need to go to the temple.
I want to give something to that child."

Pa looks at the boy sharing his meager meal.

At home Pa helps me pack a bag
with chappatis, mangoes, bananas.
From under her bed,
I take out Paati's trunk,
still full with all her things.

We give the food and the trunk to the scrawny child.

"Shiva," I say. "This is for you."

The child looks puzzled.

"My name isn't Shiva, but thanks for the food."

He opens the trunk and nuzzles his cheek against a sari.

"I can use this as a sheet," he says.

Above, I see a silver-gray cloud—

the same shade as Paati's hair.

I let her image go.

And I watch the cloud drift

like incense smoke

rising up

high.

LETTERS
and
WORDS

Waiting at home are two envelopes addressed to me.
One is in Govinda's slanted handwriting.
Inside it, I find three sketches:
the first of the lotus pond where we sat together,
the second
of two hands shaping the symbol for an eagle in flight,
the third of a boy and a girl flying a kite.
He writes:
Dear Veda,
Happy birthday.
Love,
Govinda.
My feelings leap and plunge like waves.
Plunge because his message is so short.
Leap because he remembered
and cared enough
to draw scenes of the times
our togetherness felt magical.
Stroking his signature, I reread it twice.

He called me dear. He signed love.
Does he call everyone "dear"?
Always sign with "love"?

I pluck up my courage and write Govinda a note.

> *Dear Govinda,*
> *Thanks for the birthday wishes.*
> *Let's talk sometime?*
> *Maybe we can meet at the stage beneath the*
> *banyan tree after my class, some evening when*
> *you can take a break from studies?*
> *Love,*
> *Veda*

I read my note aloud to test
whether it's enough or too little or too much.
Trying to stop worrying what Govinda will think of it,
I drop it in the mailbox.

The other card is from my old rival, Kamini.
"Veda, Many happy returns of the day, Kamini."
Kamini, whom I've almost forgotten,
remembers my birthday.
Kamini, whom I've hardly thought of,
thinks of me.
She wishes me well even though the last time we met

I was rude and left her crying
in the middle of the road.
Looking at her card, I feel self-centered.
Childish.
Anything but a year older.
I start writing Kamini a letter.
Crumple the paper, toss it away.
Look at her address, scrawled on the envelope.
Sometime after my birthday,
I'll go to her home and tell her I'm sorry.

CRESCENT SMOOTH

Pa and Ma have invited Radhika and Chandra over
in the evening for a not-so-surprise
birthday party.
Pa's bought a cake and decorated the front room.
Ma's cooked dinner.
I've prepared our entertainment:
mixed henna powder with hot lemon juice
so we can paint henna tattoos on our skin.

I ask if I may invite another guest.
"Sure," Pa says. "Even a boy."
"Your friend Govinda?" Ma suggests.
I shake my head.

I change into the blue batik skirt that ends above my knee
and walk downstairs to the Subramaniams' apartment,
my legs no longer hidden.

Shobana gazes at my outfit and gives me a thumbs-up sign,
though her mother purses her lips.

Mrs. Subramaniam probably finds my skirt too short
but at least she doesn't say so.
And she nods enthusiastically
when I invite Shobana upstairs.

Chandra offers to play henna artist.
"Birthday girl, which hand
would you like me to paint first?"
I sit in Paati's wicker chair.
Stretch out my legs.
"Feet first, please?"

She paints identical patterns on both feet,
from the tips of my toes to below my ankles.
When she's done, my feet look exactly alike,
covered with curly jasmine creepers,
hearts, lines, flowers, stars, spirals, circles.

That night, I reach under the covers.
Stroke the skin of my residual limb.
My C-shaped scar is smooth to the touch.
And it's shrunk into a crescent
thin as the last sliver of the waning moon.

SKIPPING STONE

I pause by the gate of Kamini's home.
Through a window, I see her
racing through a set of steps,
her blouse dark with sweat.
She is a pebble skipping
over the surface of a lake.
As I once was.
Not a deep sinking stone that leaves widening ripples behind
after it's disappeared.
As I hope to be.

I knock and Kamini answers the door.
"I came to thank you, Kamini.
For remembering my birthday.
For visiting me in the hospital.
It was so nice of you.
I'm sorry I never—"

"Not nice," Kamini interrupts.
"I did a horrid thing.

After you won that competition, I . . ."
She chokes up, then continues.
"I prayed something would happen so you
could never dance again.
But I never thought—I never wanted—
I'm so very sorry."

"You did what?" I say.
Kamini flinches
as though I hit her.

I didn't think anyone
could be that spiteful.
But it takes courage
to confess something like that.
I put my hand on her elbow.
"Do you really think
bad things happen
if someone prays?
I'm not sure who or what there is out there we pray to
but I doubt things work that way."

"So you forgive me?" Kamini asks.
"Sure." I shrug.
"Thanks," she says,
but her voice is hesitant, like she's having trouble believing me.

"Kamini? I'm still dancing."

"You—you are? Bharatanatyam?"

"Yes. Bharatanatyam."

"Thank God. Thank God. Veda, next time you compete,
I hope you win, I swear."

"Kamini, to me, dance isn't about competitions any longer.
And it might sound crazy,
but I'm not upset about the accident anymore.
The accident made me a different kind of dancer."

Kamini shakes her head like she doesn't understand.
But I don't know how to explain
that my love for dance is deeper.
That dance feels more meaningful now.
So I just give her hand a quick squeeze.
And she says, "I'm so glad you stopped by.
Thanks for taking the time to make me feel better."

TO TOUCH

Sitting in a chair with my students crowding around me,
I take my leg off.
Let them touch it.
As I tell them about my accident
even Uma inches forward.

"My old teacher didn't think I could dance again.
But dance isn't about who you are on the outside.
It's about how you feel inside."
I place my palms together in front of me,
symbolizing the two leaves of a closed door.
Move them apart, slowly, opening the door.
"In class, you need to shut out
sad thoughts and mean words.
So dance can let you
enter another world.
A world where you feel Shiva inside you.
Where you grow beautiful and strong and good,
because Shiva is goodness and strength and beauty."

We begin to dance.

Uma's eyes follow me around the classroom.

I should correct her.

I should direct her gaze toward her fingertips.

I don't.

Because Uma's scarf is loose around her shoulders.

Because when it slithers to the floor,

she doesn't stoop to pick it up.

Because head erect, chin lifted,

she's joined the very front row

and she's giving me an uncovered smile.

DANCING
THANKS

After the children trickle out,
I go outside and
raise my eyes to the heavens,
my palms pressed together,
thanking God for Uma's smile.

Like a farmer welcoming a long-awaited monsoon
I dance onto the empty stage
beneath the shaggy banyan tree.

A crescent moon is barely visible
in the mauve glow of the evening sky.
In it
I see the crescent caught in Shiva's matted locks.
In it
I see the crescent scar on my residual limb.

I shift my weight from one leg to the other,
turning in a circle.
Slowly.

Each green leaf above
looks purer and brighter than ever.

For my invisible audience
of the One
I
begin
to dance.

Colors blur into whiteness
and a lilting tune
that is and is not of the world
resonates within
and without me.

My body
feels
whole.

In the beat of my heart
I hear
again
the eternal rhythm
of Shiva's feet.

REACHING IN

"Good."
I look up to see Dhanam akka
standing in front of me.

"Good," she repeats.
A word I've never heard
her say to me until today.

"I am a teacher and yet
there are limits to what I can teach.
I cannot teach a student how to create
the sacred space a meditative dancer enters,
and so invites her audience to enter.
She must discover it on her own.
Alone beneath this banyan tree today
you danced without any desire for acclaim.
So your dancing feet led you
into the temple of the dancing Shiva
where they will always lead you, and those who watch,
as long as you dance for your vision of the sacred.

You carried my soul to a great height.
Thank you."

I
should be thanking
her.

"I'd like you to start
solo lessons with me," akka continues.

"But, akka—
I'm not yet—I'm not advanced enough."

"Aren't you?" Laughter
spills out of akka,
her mouth
thrown open so wide
I can see both rows of her teeth.
"There are three kinds of love, Veda.
A healthy love of one's physical self,
compassion for others,
and an experience of God.
Most of my students take decades
to experience these loves through dance.
Yet you are already starting to understand all three.
So I shall do all I can to ensure
your wish to become a dancer is fulfilled."

I want to say—do—something to thank her.
But my tongue and my hands and my head
feel too heavy with joy
to move.

"A guru is a kind of parent.
And although you are not my daughter now,
perhaps you were in a previous life.
Or will be in a future one."
Akka rests a hand briefly on my forehead.
Then she leaves.

STRETCHING AHEAD

As I leave the stage beneath the banyan tree,
I see
Govinda racing up the drive toward me.

"Veda, I got your note and I came to tell you
news I hope you'll be happy about.
I'm sorry it took me so long to share this with you
but it hasn't been easy."
Govinda's tone is nervous,
words streaming out faster than usual.
"With akka's help, I found a dance scholarship
with room and board.
I told my parents I was going to move out and take it.
My dad threw a fit.
He threatened to cut me out of his will.
But my mom sided with me
and my dad's made peace.
Maybe my finding that scholarship
finally made them both see
what dance meant to me."

"That's wonderful! I'm so happy for you!
But akka never said a word about all this.
Radhika didn't either."

"Only because I wanted to tell you myself, Veda.
I needed to work things out. Trust I'd be able to do it.
Please don't be angry—
I won't keep things from you again."

"You're always keeping things from me," I tease.
"I never knew you were a talented artist
until you sent me those sketches on my birthday."

"You liked my sketches?
Will you come with me sometime for a cup of coffee?
I'd have asked you out earlier," he rushes on,
"except I felt I didn't deserve you.
You're so strong and such a fighter.
I was always doing exactly what my parents wanted.
Until now.
So, yes or no, Veda?"

"Yes or no what?"
"Will you go out with me for a cup of coffee?"
"No."
"No?"
"I prefer tea, thank you."

FADING PHANTOMS

Govinda meets me at an outdoor café.
We sit at a table
under a pipul tree.
The type of tree that ripped up my life.
And so the tree that helped me lose
and find dance.

My limb feels hot and sweaty.
I unclick my right leg, roll the socks off my residual limb,
expose my skin to the cool breeze.

A big yellow Labrador runs over from a neighboring table
and sniffs at my residual limb.
As the dog's tail brushes against my crescent-moon scar,
my phantom limb tingles into life.
But it tickles instead of prickling with pain.
I laugh. Uncontrollably.
"What?" Govinda says. "What?"
"The dog's brought my ghost sensation back.
Except this time, my leg's tickling me."

Govinda yanks the dog away and glances
at the space below my limb
as if he's searching for my phantom.
I take his hand,
lead it to the nonexistent length of leg.
His fingers feel soft.
His fingers feel good
stroking my invisible skin.
So good I want him stroking my real skin.
Want to reach out and stroke his.
My desire scares me and I reach for the safety of my teacup.

My ghost limb fades.

Govinda lays a hand on my cheek.
I lean into his touch.
He looks shy
and almost as scared
as I was just feeling.
I burst out laughing.
Never imagined we'd share being scared
the first time we went out together.

"What's so funny now?"
"You. You look so frightened."
"I am frightened." He exhales.
Then smiles and slides
closer to me.

EPILOGUE

TEMPLE
of the
DANCING GOD:
REVISITED

Some places that sprawl in childhood memories
shrivel in size when revisited.
But the temple of the dancing God
feels just as large when I visit again,
honored with an invitation to perform there at a dance festival;
not any smaller than when I, as a child
touching sculpted feet,
first craved the gift of dance
He gave our world.

Before my performance begins on the outdoor stage,
I pour a handful of white jasmine blossoms
at the dancing feet of the bronze Shiva.
From a lofty corner a celestial dancer
smiles at me.
Beneath another curtained sanctum
where an empty space represents God as formless,
I bow; and bow to the crystal symbolizing God

as the fragmented light within us
that strengthens through each compassionate act
as our souls progress from one life to the next.

Akka's cymbals strike a crisp, clear note,
calling me to the open-air stage
where Ma, Pa, Chandra, and Govinda wait
with the rest of the audience.

I close my outward-seeing eyes and meditate
on the spot between my brows
covered by the dot of sacred vermillion.
Noises of night harmonize with the drumbeats.

Music
fills and lifts
me.

My body feels small as a speck of silvered dust
swirling upward in a cone of moonlight.

I dance
dance
dance.

Beyond
movement
for one long moment:

shared
stillness.

Then applause pierces the night
like the chirping of sparrows at dawn.
Closing my eyes to the blinding glare of the spotlight,
I salute the infinite presence within everyone in the crowd,
then slip away
until the clapping sounds as distant
as an echo from a past life.

Alone in the soft darkness of the temple courtyard,
I trace the curves of all ten perfect toes
with my fingertips.
And touch the sacred earth
beneath
both my beautiful feet.

AUTHOR'S NOTE

One of my earliest memories is of Smt. Shoba Sharma as a girl, dancing at my brother's wedding ceremony. She became a performer and dance teacher despite suffering serious physical injury. This work of fiction is inspired by her life and the lives of other dancers who overcame physical trauma, such as Smt. Sonal Mansingh, Smt. Sudha Chandran, Sri. Nityananda, and Clayton Bates (the disabled African-American tap dancer whose photograph Veda sees on Jim's wall). Smt. Kamala Lakshmi Narayanan, a child prodigy who grew into a famous performer, and Smt. Ambika Buch, an amazing teacher and exponent of the Kalakshetra school, introduced classical dance to me at an early age. My understanding of the spiritual aspect of Bharatanatyam came later, just as Veda's does in the novel. The Sanskrit verses I translated and interpreted here are taken from original texts.

Between the ages of seven and fourteen, I was privileged to have daily lessons in Carnatic music (to which Bharatanatyam dance is set) from Smt. Savitri Rajan, disciple of Veenai Dhanammal. Like akka in the novel, she never accepted payment for her lessons. This book, I hope, serves as a *guru dakshina* to her and to Sri. T. Krishnamacharya, who introduced me to yoga and Vedic chanting, and thus to the universality of spiritual truth that underlies our religious diversity.

ACKNOWLEDGMENTS

First and foremost, thanks to my brilliant, committed, and enthusiastic editor, Nancy Paulsen, who was immensely patient as this novel evolved. Nancy's ability and dedication to helping me create a story out of the flimsy chaos of early drafts is unparalleled. I am particularly glad Nancy encouraged me to experiment with this novel's form and thus to grow as a writer.

Rob Weisbach is more than an agent; he is my rock. He is critical, intelligent, humorous, generous, kind, sharp, witty, wise, and always wonderful.

Stephen Roxburgh, my most trusted "outside" reader, blessed and honored me with his steadfast belief in Veda's story. His profound insights, comments, and unswerving faith were the guiding light of her journey— from Eros, through Charis, to Agape. Thanks also to Carolyn Coman for her unstinting warmth and encouragement from the very beginning, when I started climbing the stairs as a writer.

Several poets broadened my understanding and helped in different ways: Richard Blanco, Peter Covino, Rigoberto Gonzalez, Peter Johnson, Scott Hightower.

Sincerest gratitude to the many gracious artists who took time to share with me: Sri V. P. Dhananjayan, Ahalya Bhaskar, Smt. Angelika Sriram, Smt. Bragha Bessel, Jaya Teacher, Kavya Suresh, Smt. Lakshmi Ramaswamy, Smt. Maya Shekar, Mala Ramadorai, Smt. Nithya Vaidyanarayanan, Smt. Renuka Subramaniam, Smt. Shoba Sharma, Smt. Sumitra Gautama,

Smt. Sashikala Ananthanarayanan, Sri J. Suryanarayana Murthy, Smt. Sudha Chandran, Dr. Sudha Gopalakrishnan, Smt. Sumangali Neroor, Smt. Saraswathi Vasudevan, Uma Venkatraman.

Heartfelt thanks to the generous medical personnel and persons with disabilities who spoke to me and especially to those who read a draft: Mr. Robert C. James, CPO, Mr. Joshua James, CPO, and Ms. Becky Blaine of South County Limb and Brace in Wakefield, Rhode Island; Smt. Ambika Kameshwar, director of the Rasa-Arpita Center for Theater Arts and Special Needs and the Academy for Research and Performance of Indian Theater Arts; Dr. S. Sunder, Founder and Managing Trustee, Foundation for the Rehabilitation, Education and Empowerment of the Disabled of Madras; Ms. Meena Dhadha and the staff and patients at Mukti Charitable Center, M.S. Dhadha Foundation; Mr. Michael Nunnery of Nunnery Orthotics, North Kingstown, Rhode Island; Staff of Prosthetic Artworks, LLC, Pennsylvania; Dr. Marakatham Venkatraman, Dr. Ashok Venkatraman, Dr. Venkatesh Balasubramaniam, Dr. Jeff Bachmann, Dr. Kevin Dennehy, Dr. S. Devarajan, Dr. Juergen Dolderer, Dr. Sue Ferranti, Dr. T. V. Jayaraman, Dr. S. Jay Jayshankar, Dr. Sandeep Murali, Dr. Elwira Pyz, Dr. Raman Srinivasan, Dr. Lynn Ho; John Bezak, Jeannine Atkins, Judy Begalau, Betty Cotter, Lakshmi Chayapathi, Jim Cipelewski, Kathleen Gremel, Jyoti Ganesh, Mary Heikes, Anne Herman, Maria Iacuele, Kris King, Kevin Klitze, Treacy Lewander, Sarah Ornstein, Sarah Lamstein, Emily Petit, Vicki Palmquist, Linda Pavonetti, Susanna Reich, McCall Robertson, Laurie Rothenberg, Kay Schenk, Maura Stokes, Carole G. Vogel, Maiité van Hentenryck, Sara Kreger, Jacqueline Woodson.

Finally, much more than mere thanks to my spouse, Rainer Lohmann, and our daughter, Karuna, for the love that nurtures and sustains me.

TURN THE PAGE FOR A SAMPLE OF
PADMA VENKATRAMAN'S PREVIOUS BOOK

Climbing the Stairs

The Protest March

Appa saw the crowd approaching. He pulled the car over to the side of the road and stopped. I looked at him quizzically, and he pointed.

People were marching toward us, a wall of people stretching from one end of the road to the other, filling it and spreading across both sides of the pavement, an endless mass of humanity. We could not possibly drive the car through that crowd. "Appa, is that a protest march?" I asked with excitement.

"Yes." He sounded somewhat concerned. "I didn't know they were coming this way."

I could hear their chants clearly now. "*Jai Hind!* Victory to India! Jai Hind! Victory to India!"

The bright, banned Indian tricolor flag was flapping in the sea breeze—saffron, white and green. "Freedom!" a banner proclaimed in English, Hindi and Marathi.

I watched as the flood of people came closer and closer like a rising tide. Our Austin was no more than a tiny pebble in the river of protestors who flowed around us.

"Stay inside the car, Vidya," appa said warningly, but I had already pried the door open. I stared up at a few faces, but no one made eye contact. Everyone was looking straight ahead fixedly, shouting slogans or waving flags.

As I emerged out of the car and immersed myself in the crowd, they began to sing the Indian national song, "Vande Mataram." It was a song the British had banned.

"Victory to our nation!" I shouted as loudly as I could, moving a few steps away from the car. "Jai Hind! Victory to our nation!"

Appa was watching me with a mixture of anxiety and amusement. I wanted to shout, "I'm going to college!" but that would have been inappropriate.

"We should go before amma gets worried," he said, but we couldn't. The Austin was stranded, like a beached whale. We were caught there, caught until the crowd melted away. It felt like a party. Before appa could say any more, I plunged farther in.

"Vidya!" appa shouted as I was jostled away from him by the crowd. The amusement had drained out of his face. He looked scared. "Stay close to me!"

I could barely see the top of his head. The mass of bodies between us grew thicker. I pretended I hadn't heard. At last I was a part of something important and immense. I walked farther away from him.

"Vidya! Get back here!" Appa's form was lost far behind

me. His voice was nearly drowned by the chanting. Protestors seethed around me, and I did not feel the heat of the sun on my head nor the sweat that was starting to trickle down the back of my blouse. I wanted it to go on forever.

I couldn't hear appa's firm footsteps following me. When he reached me, his grip was almost painful on my elbow, forcing me to stop, pushing me closer to the pavement. I struggled to move forward, fighting him.

Then in the distance, I heard another sound. The sound of hooves. The smell of horse sweat mingling with the acrid scent of melting tar.

I liked horses. I wanted to see the mounted police. I turned around eagerly.

The crowd had stopped moving. It was a terrible stillness— as though the sea had suddenly frozen.

"Kneel!" someone cried. "The horses won't trample us."

"Let them come! I'll never kneel before the British," another voice rang out.

Confused shouts cut through the tense air. A mounted British officer appeared and hurled out orders in a heavily accented Hindi that I hardly understood.

People were standing arm in arm, huddled together in groups or linking elbows in long chains. There was fear on some faces, anger on others, but all of them stood straight, like a grove of Ashoka trees. The brightly colored saris of a few women peeped like scattered blossoms between the drab white kurthas of the men. Their voices rose again and a Hindi song, "Sare Jahan Se Acha," trembled into the air.

As the song hung there, shivering with fear and anticipation, khaki-clad policemen charged into the crowd, their lathi sticks raised. The crisp foreign accent calling out commands in broken Hindi was coming closer.

Then I saw her. A woman with beautiful hair gathered in a glistening, thick braid that slithered down to her waist like a black cobra. I saw the veins pulsing on her neck and on her forehead. I saw the muscles flex in her arms as she lifted the tricolor flag, high, high above her head.

An Indian policeman waved his lathi at her, hesitating.

"Teach her a lesson, you squeamish fool!" the white officer on the horse yelled. "Whose side are you on?"

"Yes, sir!" the Indian policeman said, but instead of beating the woman, he turned to rain his blows down on another man.

"*Ullu ka baccha!* Son of a prostitute!" the mounted policeman cursed. The swearwords sounded strange in the officer's foreign mouth.

I heard the staccato clop of horse hooves, louder now. His stallion neighed as though in protest before the officer stooped down, his lathi landing across the woman's shoulders with a thwack. Her song was suffocated like a lamp snuffed out in a sudden wind.

The sari slipped off her shoulder and I turned away, but not before I heard the ripping sound as the officer's worm white fingers curled around her exposed blouse. I saw the immodesty of her suddenly uncovered breasts. A boy not much taller than I ran toward her, screaming incoherently.

Appa strode down the street. He lifted the lady's limp body in his arms, bending over her protectively. Blows began to fall onto his broad shoulders from the white officer's lathi.

Appa was strong. He was tall. He could have pulled the officer down off the horse, thrown him on the ground and kicked him. But he did not.

I saw the officer's arm, with its curly yellow hair, coming down, down, down on my father's head, on his neck, on his back.

Appa's blood began to creep across his light Lucknow kurtha—bright, angry, fresh and red. Not the tired rusty stain of someone else's blood. Then the lathi hit Appa's skull again, with a sound like the priest cracking open a coconut at the temple—the sound of my father's final sacrifice.

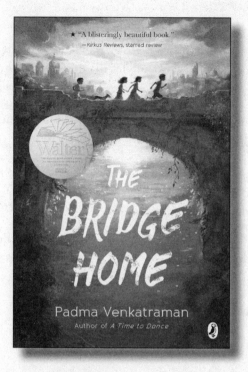

- **WALTER DEAN MYERS AWARD** WINNER
- **GOLDEN KITE AWARD** WINNER
- **GLOBAL READ ALOUD** SELECTION
- *WASHINGTON POST* **BEST BOOK**
- *KIRKUS* **BEST BOOK**
- *BOOKLIST* **EDITORS' CHOICE**

★ "A blisteringly beautiful book."

—*Kirkus Reviews*, starred review

"Viji's gorgeous storytelling makes the book sing."

—*New York Times Book Review*

★ "Breathtaking . . . A story that must be shared."

—*School Library Connection*, starred review